Sorry, Mom

Again, my mother had some advice:

"Baird is in Appalachia. Hillbilly country," she said. "This is a test, Daniel. Keep your nose clean and your pants up. Stay out of trouble for a couple of years and you'll be right back where you were in no time."

I'm not sure I wanted to be right back where I was, but, basically, it was sound advice. And I would have followed it, too. But then there was no way of knowing that a nice, friendly old couple would get murdered the first day I was there, that their sixteen-year-old foster daughter would disappear, that a snake would be set on me in my own kitchen, that someone would try to run me off the side of a mountain, that I would be shot at ... twice, and that I would fall in love with a twenty-four-year-old girl with a bachelor's degree in economics.

I really did try to stay out of trouble, Mom. I swear to God, I really did.

VIPER
QUARRY

DEAN
FELDMEYER

POCKET BOOKS

New York   London   Toronto   Sydney   Tokyo   Singapore

This book is a work of fiction. Names, characters, places, and incidents either are products of the author's imagination or are used fictitiously. Any resemblance to actual events or locales or persons, living or dead, is entirely coincidental.

An *Original* Publication of POCKET BOOKS

POCKET BOOKS, a division of Simon & Schuster Inc.
1230 Avenue of the Americas, New York, NY 10020

ISBN: 0-671-76982-0

First Pocket Books printing January 1994

10 9 8 7 6 5 4 3 2 1

POCKET and colophon are registered trademarks of Simon & Schuster Inc.

Cover art by Teresa Fasolino

Printed in the U.S.A.

*This is for
Jean Feldmeyer,
my wife and friend*

VIPER
QUARRY

My mother has always been a practical person.

On the day I was ordained a minister in the Methodist church, while other people were giving their husbands and sons inscribed Bibles and tailor-made clerical shirts, my mom took me aside and gave me some motherly advice. She hugged me and wiped her eyes with a Kleenex, and then she said this: "Daniel, you have a lot of potential. You will go far in the ministry. If you fuck around, don't do it in your own parish."

I swear to you, those were her exact words.

Then she hugged me again, cried some more, and finally ordered Uncle Dave to take some pictures of me and her standing with the bishop.

She was right, of course.

A smart son listens to his mother.

I did have a lot of potential. I went far in the ministry. And I never should have fucked around in my own parish.

1

When, after what my ex-wife calls "the big crash," I called Mom, she had only one question: "What was it?" she asked. "Money, pussy, or booze?" I suppose you could argue that this was really three questions, but I won't fault her her curiosity. I am, after all, her only son. And she has always held that these three are the demons especially assigned and commissioned in hell to lead the clergy astray.

When I told her it was all three she was neither shocked nor surprised. Her ardent faith in God and her lifelong membership in the church have kept her from becoming a fool or a prude. She has seen ministers come and go, and she knows that they are only men, weak and fallible. They are just as susceptible to pride, vanity, greed, lust, hubris, and gluttony— especially gluttony—as any man. That's why she gave me that bit of motherly wisdom on the day of my ordination.

It took me thirteen years to forget it.

In those thirteen years I managed to get married, father two children, complete my doctorate, write one book and start another, and become the senior pastor of one of the largest churches in the state. I also managed to work myself into a textbook case of burnout and a rather sleazy affair with the lady who taught the third grade Sunday school class.

A practical woman knows that there is much to be learned from scandal, Mom was all ears.

In retrospect, it seems clear that thirty-eight years old is simply not old enough to be the senior pastor of one of the biggest, most prestigious churches in the state. That position is best held by persons at least twenty to twenty-five years older. They have more experience, they have more street smarts, as it were, and they have more sermons that they can recycle and use without anyone knowing. Besides that, they are looking retirement square in the eye. If they screw up too badly, they can always say, "Fuck it. It ain't brain surgery."

If, on the other hand, you arrive at such a position at the tender age of thirty-eight, everyone knows that you are a golden boy. You are destined for greatness. This is but a pause, a rest stop on the road to the episcopacy. You will one day be a bishop, and everyone will be able to say, "I knew him when . . ."

You are, obviously, a genius. It is expected that your every sermon will be eloquent and suitable for publication. Your counsel will bring wisdom and healing to lost souls. Your decisions will be infallible, your administration brilliant, and your family life exemplary.

Let me say, to my credit, that I managed to pull it off for nearly two years. My sermons were more passionate and purposeful than those of Cotton Mather and Jonathan Edwards combined. I spent thousands of hours counseling troubled souls. I taught Bible studies, baptized hundreds of babies, and joined countless couples in holy matrimony as their mothers looked on in tears.

I sat on more boards of directors than I would have thought existed in the entire city, I sat through more meetings in a week than any human should have to endure in a lifetime, and I increased the membership of the church by a little over eight percent when mainline churches were losing members at an average of ten percent a year.

And I did it while earning a salary about thirty percent below the average take-home pay of my parishioners. It is a peculiar opinion of many large, prestigious churches that the prestige that comes with serving as their pastor will somehow pay your bills and put food on your table. So, after twenty months, I was deeper in debt than I had been when I came to the church.

My wife wasted no effort in reminding me of this fact. I was made constantly aware of the appalling state not only of our bank account but also of the house, the cars, the kids' clothing, her own clothing, and our sex life. I'm still not sure how this last item always made it onto the list, but it was there nevertheless. And deservedly so. The combination of a seventy-hour work week and an empty bank account had a devastating effect on my libido.

That is, until Ashley entered the picture.

Ashley is not her real name, of course. That is something you do not need to know, and I shall not drag her through the mud any further. Suffice it to say that she did not seduce me.

She could have, had she chosen to. She had all the right equipment. Long legs—she could not have been more than an inch shorter than my six feet. Raven black hair. Wet black eyes. A fair complexion. Small, firm breasts, and a fondness for the kind of undergarments that are usually the sole province of men's magazines. And, of course, a weakness for tall blond men who wear white collars and have a certain charisma.

It started in my office on a rainy Tuesday afternoon in March when we were supposed to be writing lesson plans for the third grade Sunday school class. She had asked for my help, as our third graders were threatening to rise in armed revolt if the boredom level of their lessons wasn't reduced significantly within the next few weeks. We met, we worked on the lesson plans, creating what I thought was a brilliant third grade survey of the Gospel of Mark, and time slipped away.

My secretary came in and said good-bye. I made coffee, and we continued our work. Thirty minutes later I was explaining my own ideas about the fallacy of the Marcan primacy theory to a rapt audience of one when she interrupted me to say, in all sincerity, I believe, "How can anyone not believe it when you say it with such passion and authority?"

Well, that did it. We fell into each others arms and then onto the couch and then onto the floor and continued in a circuit of that lavish office, using every piece of furniture we could find for purposes far beyond those for which they were intended.

The affair continued for three months, in my office, in her house, and, twice, at a Motel 6 on the other side of town.

It ended immediately after my return from the annual pastors' conference. It seems that while I was away Ashley phoned my wife and confessed her undying love for me, a love of which I knew nothing and which I certainly did not return. To this day I do not remember ever telling her I loved her, and neither do I remember her saying she loved me.

This affair was for screwing. Nothing else, I swear.

When I returned home on Friday night, all my wife had left me was my clothing, the bed, my favorite coffee pot, a cast-iron skillet, a pound of bologna, half a loaf of moldy bread, the black-and-white television from the kids' room, and a business card embossed with the name Robert Harrison, Esquire, attorney-at-law. I was to call him at my convenience.

Unfortunately, Ashley interpreted my wife's flight as capitulation—which, thinking back, I suppose it may have been—and on Saturday announced the date of our wedding—again, an event about which I knew nothing—to her best friend and singles club colleague, Laura.

Laura told her mother, who immediately called the chairman of the Pastor-Parish Committee, who called the district superintendent, who called the bishop. The bishop's call came to me while I was on the phone, trying to explain to Ashley that I had no intention of marrying her, that this had all been a big mistake, and that I was even now trying to figure out how to get my wife and kids back.

Being the busy, important pastor that I was, I had requested that the phone company supply me with Call Waiting. So I got the bishop's call at about eleven o'clock on Saturday night.

On Sunday morning my associate took the pulpit and needlessly announced my resignation. Needlessly, I say, because by this time the entire congregation knew exactly what the score was. Ashley's friend Laura substituted in the third grade Sunday school class, and presumably the boredom level plummeted to new depths. Ashley left the church never to return. My wife, whom I had finally managed to track down at her mother's house, told me to go fuck myself. One hundred and twenty-four parishioners signed a letter to the bishop pledging their support for me in "this trying and tragic time in his life." Four hundred and nineteen parishioners signed a letter demanding an immediate audit of the church's treasury and asking that all of my assets be frozen until such an audit could be completed. And my bishop called to tell me that I was an "ungrateful, insensitive, stupid, womanizing, fornicating little prick."

On Sunday afternoon I did what any modern, liberal Methodist pastor would have done in such a situation. I started what would become a seven-day bender.

My, what times those were. Seven glorious days of alcoholic oblivion. Whiskey, scotch, rye, gin, vodka, wine, and beer all taking their turn, creating an impenetrable fog through which no responsibilities, no questions, no meetings, no sermons, no Bible studies, no weddings, no counseling sessions, no baptisms, no boards of directors, could navigate. It was heaven.

An inquest was held in which eleven of my peers judged me guilty of adultery and "unfit for the professional ministry," though, as always, still "subject to the forgiving grace of a loving God."

I missed the inquest.

I was evicted from the parsonage. No problem, I was chasing away a hangover at my favorite Motel 6.

I was sought in order to give cause as to why a divorce should not be granted to my wife. I was not found. I did not give cause. A temporary separation was granted in expectation of a divorce.

Then, on the seventh day, I rested. From the drinking, that is. I spent Sunday throwing up and eating aspirin.

On Monday I had a breakfast of steak and eggs, called my wife to apologize—she told me to go fuck myself again—cleaned the three hundred and four dollars out of my amazingly unfrozen savings account, bought some clothes and a bus ticket, and headed for Louisville, Kentucky. There I called an old college friend who took me in and, in time, helped me find a job and told me to call my mother, which I did.

"So what are you going to do now?" she asked, always the practical one, my mom.

"I'm going to teach English," I told her, adding the name of the high school. "It's a private school. They'll let me teach because I have a Ph.D., even though I don't have a teaching certificate in this state."

"Where is the school?" she asked.

"Here in Louisville," I answered. Was it possible that Mom was getting a little dense in her later years? Say it wasn't so!

"I know that. Where in Louisville?" she said. No, she was being practical, not obtuse.

"In the inner city," I replied.

"Never work," she said. "You're a minister, Daniel. Just because you fucked up once doesn't mean you aren't called of God. Look at David and that tart, Bathsheba."

"Mom, Ashley wasn't a tart."

"She screwed her minister in his own office, didn't she?"

"Well . . ."

"She was a tart. But she didn't ruin your career, Daniel. This is just a setback. You apply again in two years and you'll be back in like Flynn."

And, once again, she was right.

The teaching thing didn't work at all, but it took two years for me to be convinced. The kids I taught considered proper English the "language of the white bourgeois oppressors" and simply refused to tolerate it in their presence. Shakespeare was, to their way of thinking, "a honkey faggot," and Kipling was a "mouthpiece for white imperialist oppression of the colored masses."

But it gave me something to do and paid for my

apartment and let me put a little money away and have time to apply for readmission to the ministry.

My application was accepted almost two years to the day after my ordination had been revoked, and two months later the bishop of the Kentucky Conference called to tell me he had a church for me.

Baird Methodist, Baird, Kentucky.

I told him I'd take it without hearing another word, I was that eager to get back behind the pulpit. He said to get packed, I was to be in the pulpit on the first Sunday in August. I called Mom to tell her the good news.

Again she had some advice: "Baird is in Appalachia. Hillbilly country," she said. "This is a test, Daniel. Keep your nose clean and your pants up. Stay out of trouble for a couple of years and you'll be right back where you were in no time."

I wasn't sure I wanted to be right back where I had been, but basically it was sound advice. And I would have followed it, too. But then, there was no way of knowing that a nice friendly old couple would get murdered on the day I arrived in Baird, that their sixteen-year-old foster daughter would disappear, that a snake would be set on me in my own kitchen, that someone would try to run me off the side of a mountain, that I would be shot at—twice—and that I would fall in love with a twenty-four-year-old girl with a bachelor's degree in economics.

I really did try to stay out of trouble, Mom. I swear to God, I really did.

East out of Louisville to Lexington. Then south, then east again. Drive over expressways, state highways, county roads, and roads that do nothing to deserve the name.

Wind around through the foggy green mountains of eastern Kentucky. Get lost four times. Stop and eat lunch at a place called the Blue Dot Diner where the meat loaf tastes like a soy by-product. Drive some more, through the rolling mountains. Dodge coal trucks, marvel at the beauty, and weep over what strip miners have done to it.

Ask for directions from four people who have never heard of the place and one who has. Get on Route 42 running south and keep going toward Perry, the county seat. If you get to Perry you've gone too far. Turn around and go back thirty miles, and there you are.

Baird, Kentucky. Durel County. Population of the town: eighty-eight. Population of the county ... who knows?

The town is not hard to miss. You have to want to find it.

Baird is to towns what a sandwich is to Thanksgiving dinner.

It sits in a cleft formed at the bases of three mountains. I would later learn that they were called Mount Devoux, Pine Tree Mountain, and Clark Mountain. No sign welcomes the traveler to "Beautiful Baird."

As our Appalachian Mountains are to the Alps, so Baird is to what you would normally think of as a town. You have your Baird Store, of course, specializing in soda, candy, cigarettes, chewing tobacco, bread, and bologna.

Attached to the store is the Baird Diner. Tastefully appointed with four card tables, sixteen folding metal chairs, a counter taken from a soda fountain sometime around the turn of the century, two refrigerators, a gas range, and one of those big coolers, the top of which slides back to reveal eighty-three kinds of soda.

In the back of the store is the Baird Post Office and Constabulary.

Next door is Aunt-Tiques. Old furniture piled upon itself to the ceiling. I have never seen the place open for business, and I have no idea who owns it. Neither does anyone else in town.

Across Route 42 is the Baird Volunteer Fire Department, a concrete-block building painted Florida green, and the Mountain Baptist Children's Home—administrative building, dormitories, greenhouse, outbuildings, and the original log cabin that was the home a hundred years ago. The compound sits well back from the road atop a rise that overlooks a well-groomed shaded front yard and a circular driveway.

Back across the road again are two houses used as

a camping facility for northern kids who come down here to attend work camps. A couple of little houses and, of course, the Baird Methodist Church.

My church.

I parked in front of the red brick building and estimated it to have been built sometime around the turn of the century. The cornerstone informed me that I was off by only twenty years:

BAIRD METHODIST PROTESTANT CHURCH
Congregation begun 1880
Original building erected 1890
Destroyed by fire and rebuilt
1912
Destroyed by fire. This facility erected
1920

The Methodists had dropped the "Protestant" from their name in the late 1930s, but no one wanted to replace the cornerstone, so the building had remained Methodist Protestant long after the congregation decided to change.

With their proclivity for fires, I was grateful that the parishioners had elected to go with brick on their third time out. The church was clean, well tended, if old, and really pretty nice. Inside, it was even better. Double aisles and a central pulpit told me that these folks were into preaching. No problem there. They wanted to hear the Word proclaimed. They wanted to be exhorted from the pulpit. So be it.

The maroon carpet was threadbare but clean, the candles on the altar were new, yet to meet a match. The pews were solid oak and looked uncomfortable, and there were no cushions in sight. A bad sign. The parishioners would want the service to begin and end on time. The spirit might be willing but the ass is weak.

I tried out one of the pews and found it to be well made, contoured to the curve of my back, but, as expected, a little hard on the butt. Ah, well.

"You the new preacher?"

It was a deep baritone voice, and in truth, it scared the heck out of me. I must have jumped, because the speaker laughed and strolled up next to where I sat.

"Sorry. Didn't mean to startle you. Name's Ray Hall." He extended a huge paw, and I took it in my own skinny version. His hand was beefy, callused, dry, and well muscled, but he didn't try to demonstrate his masculinity with a bone-crushing handshake. "You the new preacher?"

"Oh, uh, yeah," I said, standing and reclaiming my hand. "Daniel Thompson."

"Whadaya like to be called. Dan? Reverend? Pastor?"

"Dan's fine." I tried a smile. Good ministerial technique: always be happy unless there's something serious to be unhappy about.

He returned the smile. "But not Danny or Dano, right?"

"Even my mother doesn't call me Danny."

"Fair enough. I'm Ray Hall," he repeated.

I like it when people do that. Tell me their names several times. Most people think that if they tell the preacher their name once on Sunday morning he is duty-bound to remember it for the rest of his life. Sorry, I never had the knack.

Ray Hall stood with his hands in his pockets and looked around the church as he spoke. He was a big man, maybe six-four or six-five. Mid-fifties, steel gray hair going to white around the ears but plenty of it. He wore those gray work pants they sell at Sears and a shirt that matched. A Bic pen peeked out of his shirt pocket along with a pack of cigarettes and a disposable lighter. Sturdy black work oxfords on what had to be size fourteen feet.

"We fixed the church up and cleaned it when we heard you were coming. Some of the women insisted. Spent most of Saturday last moppin' and scrubbin'. Whadaya think?"

"It's beautiful," I said. "The windows are great." I nodded toward the two huge stained-glass windows, one on either side of the church. One was of the Crucifixion, the other of the women standing outside of the empty tomb, talking with the angel. "Are you the chairman of the administrative board or the Pastor-Parish Committee, Ray?"

He shook his head and started up toward the chancel. I followed. "Nah," he said. "Just the self-appointed welcoming committee. I hate meetings, so they don't elect me to the committees. Besides, I'm too busy, what with the store and all."

"You own the store?"

"The store and the diner. Well, May June owns the diner. It's in her name. And I'm the postmaster and the constable. It kinda keeps me busy."

"I suppose so."

"You wanna see the parsonage? I'll help you move in if ya want."

I nodded to the beat-up old VW Super Beetle sitting in front of the church. "I don't have much to move in. Just some clothes, a TV, and a stereo. I've been traveling light the last couple of years."

14

He nodded and ducked through a door behind the chancel, and I followed. We entered a small sacristy and went through another door and into what must have been the pastor's study. Another door and we were standing in the kitchen of the parsonage.

"Easy access," he said. "It ain't much but, you being single and all, you probably don't need much. Two bedrooms, office, living room, bathroom, and eat-in kitchen. You got no furniture at all?"

I shrugged my shoulders.

"Well, never mind. We'll find something for you." He handed me a ring of keys. "Well, that should do it. You gotta drive to Perry for groceries. All we got at the store is bologna and bread, milk, beer, and pop. May June makes a pretty good hamburger, though, if you want one."

I took the keys and began working them onto my own key ring as Ray looked on. He seemed reluctant to leave, but there wasn't much else to say. Finished with the key chore, I looked up and smiled. Sometimes it's best to let the other guy break the silence.

Finally he did: "What was it, Dan? Booze or pussy?"

I couldn't believe it. "Do you know my mother?" I asked while my mind raced to think of a noncommittal and innocent reply.

"Your mother?"

"She always adds money to the list, but otherwise it's virtually the same."

"Yeah, well, around here there ain't enough money to tempt anyone." He smiled. "We kinda stay with the basics."

"Well, they are that. Basic, I mean."

"I don't mean to pry, Dan, but Christ, you're forty

years old, and you got a Ph.D., you were a successful preacher, you quit to teach school for two years, and now you show up here in hillbilly heaven preachin' in a little pissant church full of old women and broken-down men."

"The district superintendent didn't tell you the whole story?" I asked.

"The D.S. don't tell us nothin' he don't have to," he said, turning to look out the window. "These little hillbilly churches are the pimples on the butt of the conference. You know they're there but you don't think about 'em very much, lest they bother you."

I couldn't help smiling at his analogy. That was just about the way I had thought of the little backwoods churches up until a month ago. But then, I had never been the pastor of one.

"The biography they gave us of you was kinda sketchy," he went on, still peering out the window. I got the distinct impression that this line of questioning was not entirely his idea. He seemed very uncomfortable. "It left a lot of holes. It wasn't so much what it said as what it didn't say. An', Dan, it didn't say a helluva lot."

I couldn't stand talking to his back, so I moved over next to him. He lit a cigarette without so much as a mother-may-I, so I took out my pipe and stoked up.

He looked surprised. "Never met a preacher that smoked," he said.

"I imagine you never met one that drank, either, did you?" I asked.

He smiled. "Well, not in front of other folks, anyway."

I laughed at that one. Ray Hall was no hick. He seemed to have an instinct for people. "Ray," I said,

"I've been driving that Vee-Dub for the past five hours without so much as a drink of water. Does the diner have a liquor license?"

He smiled again. "Nope. But the constable's office does."

I told him the whole story—the money, the pussy, and the booze—while we walked over to his store–diner–post office–constabulary and, later, while we sat in front of the little window air conditioner in his office.

When I finished the story he popped the top on a Pabst Blue Ribbon and offered it to me. I declined and sipped at mine, my first, so he made it his fourth. He took a long pull at it and leaned far back in his chair, staring at the flies on the ceiling. Then he made a great production of taking out another cigarette, a Camel, and lighting it. Tin box out of the pocket, open it, remove cigarette, close box, tamp cigarette on box, place cigarette on lip while replacing box in pocket. Fish lighter out of pocket, shake lighter, light cigarette, take deep drag, blow the smoke out while replacing lighter in pocket. Absentmindedly rebutton pocket.

Jesus! Here I was, feeling like a kid confessing to the principal that he had played hooky, and he was trying to raise his smoking habit into a sacred rite.

Finally he spoke: "Did you ever finish that second book?"

"No." I shook my head. "Almost, but not quite."

"Good. What we'll say is that you left your big church to write, and you asked for a quiet out-of-the-way little church where you could get back into the pulpit and still have the quiet and peace of mind necessary to complete the final draft. How's that sound?"

I was a little taken aback by all that verbiage. "Well,

uh, I guess it sounds fine. But if everyone's seen my biographical sketch . . ."

"They ain't. I'm the only one."

"You mean they don't know anything about me?"

"Only what the D.S. told them, and that ain't doodly." He smiled, very self-satisfied.

"How did you manage that?" I asked, still not quite sure of myself. "And why?"

He leaned forward in his chair and rested his arms on the metal desk. "The why is because I'm the constable and I wanna know what goes on in my township. We had a Baptist preacher burned out last year on accounta he preached against moonshinin'."

"Burned out? You mean someone . . ."

"Burned down his house and his church. Luckily he weren't in it. That's how they do it up here. You got somethin' against a man, you wait till he's gone to Perry for groceries and then you burn down his house."

"Jeez," was all I could think of to say.

"We've come a long way, Dan. Thirty years ago they were still shootin' revenuers up here and carryin' on family feuds."

"So you want to know if I'm gonna preach against moonshining . . ."

"Or guns or anything that might get you in trouble. Don't get me wrong. You got a right to preach again' anything you please. I just wanna know if I'm gonna have to watch over you. Now I know you, I think you'll be all right." He raised his beer can and tipped it toward mine.

No, I wouldn't be preaching against alcohol. Not with my record.

"How'd you manage to get the bio without anyone else seeing it?" I asked.

He just shook his head and rolled his eyes. "I'm the postmaster, remember? Something comes through here in the U.S. Mail, I see it first." He smiled again and sipped his beer.

"So when you saw the holes in my bio, you decided to hold on to it until . . ."

He shook his head. "Nah, that was May June's idea. She said that thing should get lost in the mail so's people wouldn't form opinions 'fore they met you. Said I ought to ask you right out what the story was. Insisted, in fact. I wasn't much up for it myself."

"You didn't seem too excited about doing it," I observed.

"Well, I wasn't. I'm not the nosy type. And don't go gettin' the wrong idea about the mail around here. Being the postmaster don't give me the right to steal and read other people's mail." He winked. "But sometimes things do get lost for a couple of days between here and Perry. You know, things like letters from church officials, eviction orders . . ."

"Dirty magazines," said a woman's voice from behind me.

I turned in my chair and was confronted by a little fat woman in a housedress and a duster. Her gray hair was pulled back into a tight bun, and she wore blue Adidas running shoes with sweat socks. She looked like the perfect grandmother from the ankles up, and she extended her hand to me.

"I'm May June Hall," she said, smiling. "This here no-account is my main man."

Ray grunted. "Shish. This here no-account is your only man or there's gonna be trouble."

"Hush up, you old coot, or I'll run off with some nice young handsome preacher man," she said, winking at me.

I took her hand and was surprised at how delicate it felt in mine. "I'm Daniel Thompson," I said. "Pleased to meet you, Mrs. Hall."

"Oh, Lord," she said, blushing. "Mrs. Hall? You hear that, Ray? This one's got manners. Not like that last one, calling everyone by their first name." She looked back at me. "But that's okay, Reverend, you just call me May June. Everyone around here does except this old cuss. He still calls me Mother."

Ray got to his feet and came around the desk. "That's what I called you for eighteen years. Old habits die hard." He swatted her ample bottom.

"Well, old men don't, so just watch yourself, mister. You invite the reverend over for dinner, or d'you just grill him all afternoon with your questions?"

"Nah, I invited him. Says he'll be glad to come over around seven." He looked at me and begged me with his eyes to confirm the time. I did. "Right now, though, we're gonna go up to the children's home yonder and see if they got some extra furniture they can lend him."

May June nodded her approval. "Okay, but I'll take care of the furniture. You gotta run over to Pine Tree Mountain. There's been another fire. Couple o' people dead."

"God A'mighty, why didn't you tell me?"

"I just did," she said indignantly. "That's what I come over here for."

He grabbed his cap and began poking around on his desk, looking for something.

"Your keys are on your belt," she told him, shaking

her head and smiling at me. "You better go, too, Reverend. If this is the place I think it is, then the dead ones may have been members of the church."

I nodded my compliance as Ray headed out the door toward a battered old Jeep. "Thanks, May June," I said hesitantly. Then I saw the biographical sketch the D.S. had sent lying on Ray's desk. I nodded to it. "For everything."

She just smiled. "Go on, now. He'll need you if there are survivors. And mind you're back by seven," she yelled as I climbed into the Jeep with Ray and we headed out of the gravel parking area. "We're havin' fried chicken and biscuits tonight, Reverend."

Ray shifted gears and turned in his seat. "He likes to be called Dan, Mother. And don't worry too much about supper. Ain't neither of us gonna feel much like eatin' if we gotta spend much time lookin' at burned-up bodies."

To become a Methodist minister you have to go through CPE. That's clinical pastoral education. It is the boot camp of the ministry.

Simply put, you spend three to six months working full-time as a chaplain in a clinical setting—a hospital, a nursing home, a mental health clinic. Usually this happens in your senior year or shortly after seminary. You work with three to ten other students under the supervision of a director.

The director is like unto God. It is his or her job to show you that your seminary education was not worth a damn when it came to teaching you how to deal with people who are hurting. CPE directors are very good at what they do.

I spent the first six months after I graduated from seminary working as a chaplain in a large urban hospital with five men and three women, all CPE students, and at the end of those six months I was completely and totally burned out.

Chaplains are truly a breed apart. They live at an emotional level that most of us experience only once or twice in our entire lives. They have the highest burnout and divorce rate of all ministerial professionals. There is, I think, something subtly masochistic about them. They must enjoy pain; they spend so much time with it.

Consider this for a moment: when, in a hospital, do the nurses or doctors call a chaplain? When a case is hopeless. When medical science cannot work a miracle. When a patient is hysterical. When a patient is uncooperative. When someone wants to know why.

Chaplains are the ones who tell young parents that their three-year-old child has leukemia. They are the ones who tell a middle-aged wife that her middle-aged husband just died on the operating table while undergoing surgery on an impacted wisdom tooth. Chaplains are the ones who sit with people and say nothing when those people have just been informed that their mother will probably die within the next hour.

It took only six months of CPE to convince me that my calling was into the local church pastorate.

My duty stations were oncology and orthopedics. But like all student chaplains I spent a number of nights in the emergency room, in the ICU, and on twenty-four-hour call.

It was the emergency room duty that opened my eyes to the promise of the local church ministry. During those times I saw gunshot wounds, knife wounds, drug overdoses, child abuse, rape, automobile and motorcycle accidents, Reye's syndrome, skin cancer, gangrene, and nearly every other vicious, brutal thing that could happen to a human body. I saw the victims and the families of the victims, and I did my pastoral duty and I went home and cried into my pillow.

Especially horrifying were the burns.

About the third week of my sojourn into modern medical technology I drew the twenty-four-hour on-call duty and got beeped during a TV football game. I drove quickly to the hospital, reported in at the desk, and was told to go immediately to the eighth floor, east wing.

Eighth floor was pediatrics.

East wing was burns.

Dear, sweet, merciful Jesus. The crying. The moaning. The heartbreaking scarred bodies of children. Twenty of them. They lay strapped to beds that looked like medieval torture devices. They were swathed in bandages and yellow ointment that covered their arms, their legs, their faces, and in one case, the child's entire body.

The ward smelled of antiseptic mixed with the sweet odor of dead human flesh.

And the crying. It assaulted you the moment you entered the scrub area, and it drowned out all but the most basic attempts at conversation. It assaulted your mind. And your heart.

I fainted before I could find the people I'd been called to help.

The next day, at the chaplains' report, I told the group what had happened, fully expecting the director to take a piece of my ass home for dinner. I had committed the first mistake of an ineffectual minister: I had allowed my personal feelings and emotions to get in the way of my duty as a pastor. He rarely showed mercy for such incompetence.

But when I finished the story he only handed me a

tissue and patted me gently on the leg. "Remember that ward," he said. "Remember it when your parishioners try to convince you that it really is important what color they paint the church parlor."

Remember it? I could not forget it if I wanted to. I still have nightmares about it, and I now have what my mother calls an unnatural fear of fire. I keep burn ointments and fire extinguishers in the kitchen, the bathroom, and the garage. I have smoke detectors in every room of the house, and I change the batteries monthly.

And even that isn't enough.

Sometimes, when I'm smoking my pipe, I will use my little finger to tamp the ashes. Sometimes the ashes aren't as dead as I thought, and I burn my finger. A small blister rises there on the tip, and it hurts like a bastard. As I suck on it and rub ointment on it, a question occurs to me: what must it be like to have this kind of burn over twenty or thirty percent of your body?

And that night I will dream of the children's burn ward, and I will wake up in a sweat and remember again how to pray.

But no nightmare, no burn ward, no amount of CPE, could have prepared me for what we found on Pine Tree Mountain on the evening of my arrival in Durel County, Kentucky.

McHenry Martin and his wife, Ernestine, were both dead, their bodies completely burned in the house fire—one body in what had been the living room of the house, the other in the bedroom.

How can I describe those bodies?

Imagine a Thanksgiving turkey baked until it is golden brown, then baked some more. Bake it until the crisp, sweet skin turns to leather. And further still until it turns flaky and begins to peel away from the bone. Most of the meat has by this time baked completely away. All that is left is dried charred bone and black flaky skin, peeling off like cheap floor tile or old wallpaper. Then let the enormous heat shrink the thing to two-thirds its size.

Now slowly transform the entire picture from a turkey into a human head.

That is what we found on Pine Tree Mountain.

(What must it be like to have this kind of burn over your entire body?)

"This'll be Mac," Ray said, stooping beside the remains in the living room. He gently turned the skull until it was facing up, and as he did so the leathery skin cracked and popped at the neck. My stomach rolled over, and the beer I'd drunk in his office threatened to come back up. My ears started to ring, and cold sweat popped out on my forehead.

"Lord" was all I could say.

"Crispy critters," Ray mumbled.

"What?"

"Crispy critters. That's what the grunts called them in Vietnam," he said, shaking his head. "I never did think that was funny."

He stood up and dusted his hands off on his pant legs. "That'll be Ernestine in the bedroom yonder. Jesus, this is a shame," he said as we started to make a circuit of the house. "They was good folks."

There was virtually nothing left of the building. Even the stone chimney had collapsed inward. The whole thing was a big pile of gray ash and black charred metal and stone. As we walked around it the ground squished under our feet where the VFD had sprayed down the yard, presumably to keep the fire from spreading. Ray said little. Occasionally he would grunt or stoop down, look closely at something, and nod to himself, but he didn't say anything to me until we were back where we'd started, in what had been the front yard.

"Okay," he said, beginning his cigarette-lighting ritual. "Let's see what the boys have to say."

The cigarette business went on as we walked toward two men who were standing in fire fighter getup by the mailbox. As I spent more and more time with Ray Hall I would learn that this was a sign that he was thinking heavily on something and did not wish to be interrupted.

Gilbert and Gaylord (pronounced GAY-lurd) Carmack were the co-chiefs of the Baird Volunteer Fire Department. Ray introduced us and we shook hands all around, but it wasn't until they took off their fire hats that I realized they were identical twins. Possibly the ugliest identical twins in the entire world.

They were as tall as Ray, painfully thin, and they both had Ichabod Crane necks and heads. Their haircuts were as unflattering as possible, though I suppose trying to make some part of these guys attractive with a pair of barber shears would have been like trying to press a lump of coal into a diamond with your bare hand. Their hair was cut high above their enormous ears, bobbed around halfway up their skull in back, and left to bangs on their foreheads.

From the middle of their bony faces protruded hawk noses that curved down so far they might have touched their chins ... had they possessed chins.

It seemed sad enough that there should be a single person so homely in the world, but twins ... The single thing that differentiated them was that Gaylord held his chewing tobacco in his left cheek and Gilbert held his in his right. The appearance of these large lumps on their faces did nothing to soften the overall effect.

The brother named Gaylord separated his hand from mine, spit, and said, "So you're the new preacher." His voice was a pleasant baritone, but he spoke so slowly I wondered if he would ever finish the sentence.

"That I am," I said, smiling, but trying to seem humble.

"Whadaya doin' hangin' out with this here no-account?" Gilbert said, spitting in Ray's general direction. His speech was indistinguishable from his brother's.

"He just got in a while ago. May June gave me this address, and I brought him along. I figured it was the Martin place," Ray said.

The Carmacks considered this for a moment and must have decided it was enough of an answer for them.

Gaylord spit again. "Church clean enough?"

"It's beautiful," I said.

"Oughta be," Gilbert said. "Our wives spent near all o' Saturday cleanin' the place." He spit again.

Now I got it. The second way to identify them: Gaylord spit before he spoke, as though announcing that something of significance was about to be said. Gilbert spit after he spoke, using a sort of expectorative punctuation. I hoped I would never have to talk to these guys when they weren't chewing.

And wives? God does work in mysterious ways. That one so homely should find a mate would have surprised me. That both had been so lucky left me absolutely awestruck. My belief in miracles was restored.

"They done okay?" Gilbert asked.

"They really did a fine job."

"The house too?"

"The house is great. I couldn't ask for more."

"Well, you could ask," Gaylord said, smiling with stained teeth that were too straight to be his own. "But 'twouldn't do no good."

They both laughed at that. Didn't laugh, exactly, just sort of chuckled and looked at each other with raised eyebrows. Point for our side, brother. We won a little word game with the city slicker preacher.

I laughed too. I've found that it doesn't pay to play get-backs. Let them win one and be nice about it. Who's hurt?

Ray crushed his cigarette under his boot, his thinking done for the moment, and stepped forward. "One o' you comedians want to tell me what happened here?"

Again the twins looked at each other, and some sort of silent communication seemed to take place. At last Gaylord spit dangerously close to his own foot and said, "Call came in about one o'clock this mornin'. Time we got here the thing was damn near gone."

"Who called it in?" Ray asked.

"Don't know. Just a voice on the phone. 'They's a fire up on Pine Tree.' An' he hung up."

"It was a man's voice?"

"Well, sure. I reckon it was, now you say."

"Okay, then what?"

"Well, I set the alarm to ringin', and a couple o' the boys come, an' we come a flyin' up here. Gil and a couple others come up in the amb'lance here." He pointed to the old ambulance parked half off the road across from us.

"So when you got here the place was near gone and you didn't try to put the fire out," Ray went on for him. I got the feeling people did that a lot for the Carmacks. Otherwise their stories might never get finished.

"Shit, Ray. She was burnin' to beat the band." He gave me a glance. "Sorry, Reverend."

"He's heard it before, Gay. So what'd ya do?"

"We sprayed down the yard to keep it from spreadin's all. Good thing ol' Mac kept the yard cleared way back like he done, or we mighta lost the whole damn mountain. Sorry, Reverend."

I nodded and winked: it's okay, I'm not shocked. I hate it when people apologize for being themselves around a minister. Generally I'll try to find some way to put them at ease and get them to stop worrying about trying to impress the pastor. At the moment all I could think of to do was take out my pipe and light it.

By this time Gilbert could no longer keep silent. He looked at me as he spoke. "Gotta keep the yards cleared back like that," he said, pointing. "Keeps the copperheads away from the house." Spit.

"They get under the house you can't hardly get 'em out," Gaylord added. "I knew a guy once tried to smoke 'em out an' burned down his entire house."

"You never did," Gilbert said.

"I guess I did. Ol' Bernerd Pitkinson's the one. Burnt up his whole damn house," Gaylord insisted.

Gilbert shook his head. "Well, I'll be damned."

Then, as though he was just making sure: "He did that goin' after copperheads?"

No answer. Gaylord just spit and nodded his head.

Ray cleared his throat in an attempt to bring them back to the subject. "So you just wet down the yard and let it burn, is that it?"

"Yeah," Gaylord said, once again the spokesman. "Burned most of the night and then smoldered through the day. 'Bout an hour ago we commenced to lookin' through it like we're supposed to. That's when we found Mac an' Ernie. We sent the other boys on home with the truck an' waited for you."

"Damn shame," Gilbert said. "Martins was good folks."

"How you know it's them?" Ray asked.

Without comment Gaylord walked across the road to the ambulance and came back. "Found this," he said, holding out a big charred western belt buckle. "It was layin' aside the body in front there. Back yonder's the bedroom. Figured that had to be Ernie in the bed."

Ray took the buckle, looked it over, and handed it to me. It was scarred and black from the fire, but when I rubbed it with my finger and thumb it proved to be a nice piece of Indian silver with a big chunk of turquoise in the middle. The name "Mac" was raised on the surface.

"You move the body?" Ray asked the twins.

"Naw," Gilbert answered. "That buckle was layin' next to him, kinda wedged up close but not right under. Christ, Ray, we done this before. We know better'n to move a body before you give us the okay." Then, looking at me: "Sorry, Reverend."

"Anything else?"

"Just this here," Gaylord said, producing a piece of thick cedar siding about the size of his hand. "We figure the fire was set."

Ray took the piece of siding and showed it to me. It was charred on one side but relatively clean on the other. "See here," he said, pointing to the charred side. "Burned on the outside, but"—he turned it over—"clean as a whistle on the inside."

I didn't get it, and he read the confusion in my expression.

"Cedar burns fast but not hot. Some of this siding was new and still kinda green. Mac cut it and put it on himself. Whoever started the fire poured something around the outside of the house—probably gas or kerosene—and lit it. It burned too fast to really catch these green boards, but the older ones went up okay. When the house collapsed, the walls fell in and protected the inside surface of the board while the fire raced to the center of house where the wood was the oldest."

I was a little surprised at his expertise. "You learned all that where, constable school?"

This set off another round of chuckling from the Carmack twins. Score one for the preacher.

A look from Ray silenced them. "I learned it from looking at over a hundred burned-down schools, houses, barns, and other buildings in the past four years. Arson's our favorite pastime around here. Haven't you heard?"

"An' the army," Gaylord said gravely. "Ray here was an MP in the army. Ain't that right, Ray?"

"Yeah, Gay. I had a lotta arson cases to investigate when I was an MP in Kansas and Pennsylvania. Jesus."

Gaylord looked sideways at me, thought about apologizing for Ray, and decided against it. A wise choice, I thought.

Ray sighed and ran his hand through his hair. "If the house was already fully engulfed by the time you got here, the fire must have started around, what, twelve, twelve-thirty?"

The Carmacks looked at each other, communicated silently again, then nodded simultaneously.

Ray nodded in response. "Any ideas what Mac was doin' in the living room at midnight?"

Gaylord looked as though he'd been waiting to be asked. "Well, now you mention it, we did give that some thought. See, he ain't really in the living room. He's more in the doorway."

"Like he was kinda layin' across the ... whadaya call it?" Gilbert added.

"The threshold?" I offered. So far I had not offered much in the way of help, so I thought I would jump in. Preachers are, after all, good with words.

"That's the word," Gilbert said. Was that respect I saw on his homely face? "Sorta like he was layin' 'cross the threshold there."

"Face down," Ray added.

"Yessir," Gaylord said. "Kinda curious, ain't it? You figure someone coldcocked him, Ray?"

"Not on the head. His skull's intact. They mighta hit him hard enough to knock him out without breaking the skull, though."

Gaylord spit toward the ashes of the house. "But that would mean he was goin' in the house when someone hit him. So what was he doin' outside at twelve-thirty in the A.M.?"

"Back to square one," I said.

"Maybe we oughta ask the girl," Gilbert said.

Everything stopped. Ray and Gaylord looked at Gilbert as though he had dropped his pants. After a long moment Ray said, "What girl?"

"That girl they had livin' here with 'em. The one from Mountain Baptist."

"They had a kid from the children's home living here?"

"Yeah, sure. I thought you knew."

Gaylord looked as though he had been kicked in the stomach. "He knew! I didn't even know, and I'm your own kin." Obviously he was not accustomed to his brother having some knowledge that he didn't, and he didn't like it one bit.

"Well, hell, Gay. It just never came up is all." Gilbert kicked the ground like a little kid caught at cheating in a game of marbles.

"What was her name?" Ray asked. "How old was she?"

"I don't know her name. An' she weren't no child. She was sixteen. 'Least that's what she said. Said they kicked her outta the home an' she was crashin' at Mac an' Ernie's place." Gilbert still didn't look up.

"When did she say this?" Ray asked.

"Saturday a week. I give her a ride from the foot o' the mountain. She was walkin'."

"What'd she look like?"

"Nice lookin', in a wild kinda way. Tall, blond, skinny. Big eyes. Smoked Marlboros and cussed like a sailor. She was a wild one all right."

Gaylord sighed. "Gil, you just described half the teenage girls in this county. What made her so different?"

"Well . . ." He hesitated, stalling.

"For chrissake, Gilbert," Ray said, losing his patience long after a mere mortal might have.

"Well, she said she'd show me her titties if I'd give her a ride up here, is all." This he said faster than anything he'd said since Ray and I got to the site. Maybe faster than anything he'd said in his life. Then, "Sorry, Reverend."

Ray forced the impatience out of his voice. "He's a man, Gil. He knows about titties."

"Yeah, well . . ."

"Did she?"

"Did she what?"

"Did she show you her titties, ya idjit!" Gaylord snapped.

"I reckon she did."

"Well?"

Gilbert finally looked up, first at me, then at Ray, then at his brother. He smiled shyly. "Not bad. Bigger'n you woulda thought for such a skinny little thing." His smile faded quickly. "You ain't gonna tell Chelsea, are you, Gay?"

"Hell no, I ain't gonna tell Chelsea. She may be your wife, but I gotta sleep with her sister."

Good Lord, they were married to sisters. Somehow they had managed to find two sisters as homely as they were. Only in America.

As this went on, Ray had been performing his cigarette ritual. Now he blew out the smoke and said, "So, now that we've seen her titties and got you both back in the good graces of your wives, you wanna tell me where she is?"

They looked at each other again and shrugged at the same time. "Search me," Gilbert said.

"You think maybe she done it, Ray? Set the fire an' all?" Gaylord asked.

Gilbert uncharacteristically spit before he spoke. "Nah, she didn't do it. She was wild and all, but she weren't no killer. Maybe whoever done it carted her off."

Gaylord spit, reclaiming his rightful position in the family. "Or maybe she seen what happened and got away. Maybe she's up there on the mountain, lost or somethin'."

"Or maybe she's over there," Ray said, nodding toward the ashes of the house.

The Carmacks looked at each other. They had not considered that possibility. Then they shook their heads. Once considered, they rejected it as absurd.

"Naw," Gaylord said. "If she was in there, we'd've found her. Nope. Onliest ones in there is Mac and Ernie."

"What makes you think the one in the back is Ernie?" Ray asked.

Gilbert looked shocked. "Well, that's where the bedroom was, weren't it? Who else would be in Mac an' Ernie's bed but . . . Oh, I see."

Gaylord was aghast. "Well, now, that's just horseshit pure and simple. McHenry Martin wasn't perfect, but he weren't about to throw his wife out and jump into bed with some little sixteen-year-old whore who shows her titties to ugly old men for a ride up the hill. That's just—sorry, Reverend—horseshit."

"Get off your high horse, Gay," Ray said. "I'm just considerin' possibilities."

'Well, that ain't even a possibility as far as I'm—"

"You're probably right. We'll know soon as you two get the bodies into Perry and the coroner runs a dental check. In the meantime, let's just keep all the details here between the four of us, okay? No need gettin' folks all worked up." Ray started off toward the remains of the house. "While you're takin' care of Mac an' Ernie, me and the preacher here will just nose around a mite. Make sure we didn't miss her." He looked back at me. "You comin'?"

I did not want to go. I did not want, on the day of my arrival in Durel County, to spend the waning hours of that day poking around in a mountain of ashes, looking for a third charred body.

But I went.

And I said a little prayer that we wouldn't find the girl here. That, instead, we would find her on some mountain road flashing her surprisingly big titties at some other homely old stranger in exchange for a ride.

Whoever said there are worse things than death hadn't seen the bodies of McHenry and Ernestine Martin.

37

4

Sometimes prayers get answered.

We didn't find another body in the ashes of the Martin house. We sifted and poked and prodded for more than an hour, and when we were done, we looked like two sweaty coal miners emerging from the mines after a day's labor.

The water from where the firemen had soaked the yard combined with the wood ash from the house to ruin my Nikes, and my cutoffs and T-shirt were lost causes. Ray's gray workman's uniform was shot, too.

We climbed into the Jeep without a thought for the torn upholstery and headed back down the mountain. It was after 7:30 P.M. when we pulled up in front of the diner, but the sun was still just above the mountains and the big Nehi thermometer in the shade of the porch read 87 degrees.

"Lord God, look at you two," May June said from inside the screen door. "Well, chicken or no chicken, you ain't comin' in here looking like that."

Ray looked tired, dirty, and a little miffed. I certainly wouldn't have messed with him looking like that. "Mother, we're hot and tired and we need something cold to drink, and then maybe we'll be ready to think about some dinner."

She pushed open the screen and handed us two ice-cold Budweisers. "Here. Drink these and take a shower. I'll keep your dinner."

Ray sat in a lawn chair that I would have junked last summer, and I sat on a straight-backed chair that looked as if it had come from my grandmother's dining room set. We drank our beers and smoked in silence and watched the shadow of the mountain behind us make its way across the road and up toward the Mountain Baptist Children's Home.

When Ray threw his cigarette butt into the road I thought it would be okay to talk.

"So what do you think happened?" I asked. I did not have even the slightest idea, just a ball of confusing information in my mind.

He held up his hand and counted on his fingers as he talked. "Fire started between twelve-thirty and one in the morning. Mac layin' in the doorway, face down, head in the house. Ernestine still in her bed."

"I don't understand the significance of Mr. Martin being in the doorway," I said, admitting my ignorance. I have found that people who might otherwise be reticent are willing to talk if they can do it in the role of teacher.

"Mac was goin' into the house when he fell."

"Yes, well . . . ?"

"A man doesn't go into a burning house."

"Maybe he does if his wife is sleeping in one of the

back rooms." I had seen the scarred arms and faces of parents who had tried to save their burning children.

"Maybe, but not likely. Mac loved Ernie, no mistake, but he wasn't a fool. See, Preacher, these houses up here are all made of pine. They burn hot and fast. Mac knew that. He never woulda tried to get back into that house."

Ray seemed to be rolling now, so I said nothing.

"The house was set afire, see. It didn't start burning gradual and then take off. It was fine one minute and completely swallowed in flames the next. Whoever done it poured gasoline or kerosene all the way around the house and lit it. The burn was even all the way around.

"Mac never woulda gone into a house burnin' like that, no matter how much he loved Ernie. Also, we'd have to ask what he was doin' outside at midnight. And how'd he happen to fall just inside the door there?"

"So you think someone killed him first and then set the fire?" I asked.

"Yeah. I think ol' Mac had it out with someone on the front porch or in the front yard. I think he turned on his heel and started to walk back into the house and someone coldcocked him as he was goin' in the door. Killed him. Probably didn't mean to, but once it was done, he had to hide it. Panicked. Poured some fuel around the house and lit it and took off."

I shook my head. "Ray, that's just speculation. There's no proof of any of that. You said yourself that Mr. Martin's head wasn't hurt."

Ray stood and stretched. "I said it wasn't busted. That don't mean he wasn't hit. It is curious, though, now you mention it. That's the only part that don't fit."

"What about the girl?" I asked, standing up next to him.

"Yeah, that's the other curious thing. Either she saw it and ran off or she done it herself. Or she knows who done it and is with him now."

"Or none of the above," I mumbled.

"Huh?"

"Nothing. Just thinking to myself."

"Yeah. Well, we'll just have to ask Dr. Sites about her, I guess. Let's get cleaned up and have some supper."

We? We were going to ask Dr. Sites? Why *we?* I was just the new preacher in town. I was trying to keep my nose clean, not get involved in a murder investigation.

Really, Mom. I did not want to get mixed up in this thing. It was Ray who pulled me into it. But then, how could I refuse a man whose wife made fried chicken and biscuits and kept her Budweiser in the crisper of the fridge?

I went back to the parsonage, dug my suitcase out of the VW, showered, and was back at the diner in forty minutes. Fried chicken, buttermilk biscuits, home fries, green beans with ham chips, and another cold Bud were all waiting for me on the scarred counter.

While I ate my third chicken thigh I learned that Dr. Sites was the administrator of the Mountain Baptist Children's Home. May June had called him and arranged for me to borrow some old furniture from one of the dorms until I could get to Perry and buy some of my own. I was to pick it up that evening, or, if I wanted to stay the night with her and Ray I could get it in the morning. I was exhausted from the drive, the discovery of the bodies, the conversation with the Carmack twins, and the huge meal. I was perfectly willing to wait until Friday morning to get the furniture.

Ray said, "We'll go over right after we have our coffee. We got some business to discuss with the good doctor anyway."

So, at a little after 9:00 P.M., with the sun making a spectacular show of itself behind the mountains to our backs, we walked up the driveway to the Mountain Baptist Children's Home.

The administration building was a giant two-story plantation house with a false front that, judging from the look of it, was rarely used. A broad, slightly raised porch ran the complete length of the building, and four huge columns gave the illusion of strength and power.

The whole image was belied, however, by ten or twelve broken-down lawn chairs of various kinds and colors lying on the floor of the porch and propped up against the building. The big double front doors appeared to be painted shut.

From the road, some twenty or thirty yards away, the place looked formidable and imposing. As we grew closer, it looked old and worn out. The sides and back of the big building were not brick, like the front, but concrete block painted with a thousand coats of glossy white lacquer. Maybe a fifth of the window-panes were cracked or broken, and the grass in the front yard, upon close inspection, turned out to be not grass at all, but a collection of hardy weeds that had managed, somehow, to survive the hot, dry summer.

The driveway circled up from both sides to the back of the building, and as we followed it around the corner, a huge pear-shaped man in bib overalls and a Beechnut Chewing Tobacco cap met us. His eyes were set far apart, and there was in his face just a hint of those characteristics usually associated with Down's syndrome.

"Hey, Ray," said the giant, coming toward us. His voice was high-pitched and a little nasal.

"Hey, Darnell," Ray said. "Meet the new Methodist preacher. Daniel Thompson. Likes to be called Dan."

Darnell extended his hand, "How ya doin', Reverent Dan."

"This here's Darnell Kody," Ray said. "Darnell's the caretaker and handyman here. That right, Darnell?"

Darnell smiled and nodded. "Yeah."

"You ever need something fixed," Ray went on, "you just ask Darnell here. He's got hands made for fixin'. Ain't that right, Darnell?"

Again, "Yeah."

I could tell Darnell was embarrassed by Ray's compliments, so I tried to change the subject. I pointed to the burlap bag in his hand. "You on trash pickup duty, Darnell?"

He shook his head. "Nah. Kids here do that."

"Ah. Well, I saw the bag and—"

"Copperheads."

Jesus!

"You got copperheads in the bag?"

"Just one. He come out and I got 'im." Darnell looked up and smiled. He held the bag out to Ray. "You wanna see him, Ray? He's a big 'un."

Ray pulled a face and stepped back. "No, that's okay, Darnell. You just go on an' let 'im go."

Darnell shrugged. "Okay." And off he went, down the driveway.

Ray called after him. "Where'd you get 'im?"

"Under the porch," Darnell yelled without looking back. "Whole mess of 'em under there."

Ray raised his voice another notch and hollered one more time. "Is the reverend in?"

Darnell just raised his hand over his head and waved it back and forth.

"Is that yes or no?" I asked.

"Beats me." Ray laughed. "Probably didn't hear me. He's okay. I meant what I said about fixing stuff. Darnell don't have much going for him, but he has that. I think the good Lord gives folks like him a little extra sometimes, you know. Just to even things out."

I said that, yes, it did seem that way. But I was lying. I'd seen too many hurt, crippled, retarded, sick people in my life to believe that anything, any little talent they might have, could compensate for the suffering they had to endure. Some people are just unlucky and that's all there is to it. Shit happens, as the bumper sticker used to say. And sometimes there's nothing you or God can do about it. But it's a hard thing to explain standing in a driveway, so I let it pass.

We walked on around to the back of the administration building, in through the kitchen, out of the kitchen into a dining room, smaller than I had imagined, and up a flight of stairs to a small landing with a fake potted plant and three doors. Ray was just about to knock on one of the doors when a handsome man of about forty-five opened it.

"Oh, Lord! You startled the bejesus outta me,

Ray," he said. He was dressed in stone-washed jeans, checked shirt, and running shoes. His hair was razor-cut, with just the right amount of gray at the temples to give him credibility.

"Sorry, Jerry. Just wanted you to meet the new Methodist preacher. This here's Dan Thompson," Ray said.

Jerry offered his hand and I shook it. The grasp was firm and confident, the palm dry. Being a preacher, I shake a lot of hands and I've learned that the impression they make is often pretty close to the mark. I liked Jerry Sites's handshake, so I liked him.

Ray said, "Dan, this here's the Reverend Doctor Gerald Sites, Administrator of Mountain Baptist Children's Home."

Jerry Sites laughed. "Ray knows how I love to be called by my full title, how it impresses everyone around here."

"Shit," Ray said under his breath.

"See?" Jerry said. "Don't grovel, Ray. It's embarrassing." Ray smiled and shook his head. "I guess you fellas are here for the furniture. May June called earlier and I told her you could take anything you wanted out of the boys' dorm."

"The boys don't like the furniture?" I asked.

"Well, I suppose they would if we had any. Boys that is. We have a dorm built for forty and we're housing eight, so we got more furniture than we know what to do with. Don't worry, if I have a sudden need of it I'll call you and let you know."

"Dorm unlocked?" Ray asked.

"No. It's one thing to loan furniture out to a fellow pastor," Jerry said. "It's another thing to have it stolen by someone who's just gonna take it into Perry and

45

sell it at the used furniture store." He held out a key ring with about a hundred keys on it for Ray. "Here. I don't know which one it is. Happy hunting."

Ray took the keys and fumbled with them for a moment. "Reverend Sites, can we talk for a minute?"

The sudden seriousness seemed to take the administrator by surprise. He seemed uncomfortable, some of his self-confidence shaken. "Well, uh, sure." He turned and went back into his office, flipping the light switch as he went.

The office decor was probably best described as up-scale secondhand: a big oak desk with a glass top, wooden desk chair that squeaked and swiveled, three plain straight-backed chairs. There were diplomas and photographs of children on two of the walls. One wall was a giant blackboard with "Things to Do" written across the top; the other wall was all windows.

Jerry sat down at his desk. "Is something wrong, Ray?"

"Well, I'm afraid I got some bad news."

Jerry Sites's face went completely blank. "One of the kids in trouble again? What is it? Vandalism? Stealing?"

"No, nothing like that. It's the Martin family, up on Pine Tree Mountain." Ray let his voice come up at the end so it sounded like a question.

Jerry nodded.

"Their house burned down last night. They're both dead."

"Oh, Lord." Jerry Sites seemed to shrink a little behind the desk. "LeAnn?"

"That the girl that lived with 'em?" Ray asked.

Jerry nodded again.

"Well, we don't know. The bodies were burned

pretty bad. One we're pretty sure was Mac. We think the other one was Ernestine. We didn't find any other bodies."

"You *think* the other was Ernestine?"

"Well, it was in the bed. The sheriff's office in Perry's doing the autopsy and checking dental records. They'll probably let us know next week sometime. But right now we're assuming the other body was Ernie."

Jerry shook his head. "Lord God."

"The thing is, Jerry, we don't know what part the girl played in this thing." Ray took out a cigarette and held it.

"What part she played? Whadaya mean, Ray?"

"It looks like Mac and Ernie were murdered, Jerry."

"And you think LeeAnn did it?" No indignation or surprise. Hardly even a question. More of a statement.

"Well, I ain't saying that. I'm just saying that she's missing and I'd like to talk to her."

"Mm." Jerry looked at me and raised his eyebrows.

"I'm just here for the furniture," I said.

"Mac and Ernie were members of Daniel's church," Ray said. "He's an interested party. Can you help us, Jerry?"

He leaned back in his squeaky chair and sighed. "I guess she coulda done it. She was capable enough."

Her name was LeAnn Bertke and she was sixteen years old. Jerry Sites removed a folder from one of several filing cabinets in his office and browsed through it as he spoke.

"She came here four years ago. That is, I brought her here. We got reports that her daddy was abusing her, and me and Don Merriweather drove over and picked her up." He looked up from the file folder at me. "Donny was your predecessor. Real nice fella."

Ray asked, "How was she being abused?"

"Sexually, we think. Never did prove it, but she was in bad enough shape that we could take her at our own discretion." He thumbed through the file. "See, her daddy was one of those self-ordained Holy Roller preachers. Had a little church back in the mountains where they handled snakes and drank rat poison and what have you. Crazy.

"Anyhow, one of the teachers over to the school, Mrs. Causey—she's dead now—came to me and said

48

how little LeAnn had something wrong with her. I met with the principal and we talked to LeAnn, and she told us the whole story.

"Her daddy was making her drink poison in church and not feeding her and beating up on her. He said he was beating the devil outta her, something like that. She had bruises all over her right arm and leg, and her nose had been broken."

"What was her mother doing all this time?" I asked.

"Mother ran off when she was just a toddler, she said. Just about the time her daddy got laid off at the mine and took up preaching."

"Good for her," I said. How is it that Christianity can be such a kind and gentle religion and such a mean and hateful one at the same time? Hospitals and nursing homes, crusades and witch burnings—they all come in the same package.

"What happened after the mother took off?" Ray asked.

Jerry looked up from the folder. "Well, we only have the girl's word for it, you understand. But according to her, everything went along fine for five or six years. Her daddy preached and did a little farming, and they got along okay.

"Then, when she was nine or ten, he got saved by a traveling revivalist and decided he hadn't been preaching the true Gospel. Went off the deep end and started handling snakes and all. That's about the time he started screwing her."

"Jesus," Ray said. "Her own father."

"Yeah. He called her his little princess. Then he took to calling her his whore. Little Babylon the whore. He was a sicko."

"And this went on for how long?" I asked.

"Three or four years. We're not sure. We found out when she was twelve. Me and Donny got a court order and went down and got her. We were lucky; the old man wasn't home. House was a mess. Rats, bugs, lice. Garbage everywhere. Cages full of snakes. Lord."

"What was his name?" Ray asked.

Jerry looked back into the file. "Zester. Zester Bertke. I won't dignify him by putting 'Reverend' in front of it."

"He give you any trouble?" Ray asked.

"Oh, for a while, yeah. Came around threatening and screaming. Nothing direct, you understand. Just calling down the wrath of God on all of us. Scared poor LeAnn near to death."

"What happened to him?"

The administrator shrugged. "Don't know. Donny told him if he didn't take off and leave us alone, he'd have him arrested for child abuse and neglect. Then he said maybe he'd just save the taxpayers some money and whip his ass himself."

"The Methodist minister said that?" I asked, a little shocked. Most of us are lovers, not fighters.

Ray chuckled. "That sounds like him. He was a big old boy. Probably used them hands plenty before he started preaching."

"He was an ex-marine, 'bout your size and coloring, maybe a little heavier," Jerry said to me. "Got saved by a Methodist preacher in the service. Quit, went to college and seminary, and got ordained when he was thirty-eight."

"So Zester Bertke just took off, is that right?" Ray asked, getting back to the subject.

"Yeah," Jerry said. "One of his parishioners was up here a few months later visiting one of her kids, said

50

he'd gone off to Nashville to join up with the Jimmy John Swaysgood Crusade, though I don't think even Jimmy would have him. Jimmy John's crazy, but not that crazy."

Jimmy John Swaysgood was an independent Baptist evangelist whose home base was in Nashville. He had a syndicated television show, a radio show, a magazine, a huge church, and was thinking about starting a college. Money, of course, was a major recurring theme in Jimmy's sermons.

Ray shifted in his chair. "Jerry, you said the girl coulda set the fire."

Jerry Sites leaned back in his chair and rubbed his temples. "I'd better call Rachel and tell her I'm gonna be late," he said.

He used the phone on his desk to call his wife, but from his end of the conversation I could tell that it wasn't really a necessary call. Ministers' wives learn that their husbands are like cops—on call twenty-four hours a day, seven days a week. Family plans and events often have to be put on hold because a parishioner has had a heart attack or a baby. Unexpected phone calls in the middle of the night are commonplace, and late hours are the rule rather than the exception.

While Gerald Sites was not a parish pastor, I imagined his duties were not dissimilar to mine. If anything, they might have been even more demanding.

More likely, there was something about LeAnn Bertke that he didn't enjoy discussing and this was a stall to let him figure out a delicate way of talking about it.

Finally the call was over and he looked back at us. "Well, she understands. But she's not happy."

Ray and I said nothing. It's always uncomfortable to hear someone bitch about his or her spouse. You don't know what to say. There's nothing to agree with, and you feel like a fool if you sympathize. It was Ray who broke the uncomfortable silence.

"You were gonna tell us about LeAnn," he said.

Jerry Sites leaned back again. I was learning that this was his thinking posture. He sighed deeply. "LeAnn Bertke was one of my failures," he said, looking at the front of his desk. "We did everything we could for her, but none of it worked. I think her daddy screwed her up too bad to be fixed."

He fell silent for a long time, maybe two or three minutes. When he spoke again, it was as though those past events were all taking place again in front of his eyes.

"We took her away from that place and that monster, and she spit in our faces. She was a lost cause before she ever got here. I just wish we could have seen it earlier."

"She caused trouble?" I asked.

"That's not uncommon among sexually abused children. She was sexually advanced for her age. Seductive, I guess you'd say. She was twelve, thirteen years old and she came on to her teachers, the house parents, the boys here at the home, even me. That was the only way she knew how to get what she wanted."

"Anyone take her up on her offers?" Ray asked.

Jerry shrugged. "Probably. We never caught them, but it's hard to believe someone didn't take advantage of her. She was an attractive girl. An early developer. She was tall for her age, thin, but with a good figure, and she had a naturally clear complexion. Her teeth weren't bad, either, which is unusual for a lot of these kids."

"You got a picture of her?" Ray asked.

Jerry slid a five-by-seven color glossy and an old Polaroid photo from the file and handed them across the desk. I stood up and leaned over to get a look and saw, in the five-by-seven, a fairly attractive teenager who had refused to smile for her official school portrait. She had a tough edge, but there was something seductive in her eyes—or maybe I just expected to see it there after listening to her guardian.

The Polaroid was of the same girl years earlier. The right side of her face was bruised and swollen. Her nose, too. I felt a lump in my throat and sat back down quickly.

"Oh, yeah," Ray said. "I seen her around."

"Hard to miss her the last year. Never wore underwear. Halter tops, tube tops, tank shirts, blue jean shorts cut up to heaven. Last year I spent half my time driving to Perry and back to pick her up. She'd get outta school and then go hang out with some creeps instead of coming home. I guess that's where she picked up smoking cigarettes."

"She pick up anything else in Perry?" Ray asked.

I didn't know what he meant, but I suppose he was figuring that with a reputation like hers she might have gotten a dose of the clap.

Jerry nodded. "Coupla times she came home with reefers. I just took them away from her and threw them out. Hardly seems worth the fuss anymore," he said to me.

"Most folks around here, if they want pot, they grow their own," Ray said by way of explanation. "It's the new moonshine, though we got some of the old kind, too." Then, to Jerry, "Did she ever come on to you on these rides?"

"Oh, hell, yes, Ray. The girl was a whore. If she wanted something, she flashed her boobs and a smile. She'd have slept with a rattlesnake if she thought there was something in it for her." The minister's sympathy seemed to be eroding.

"That why you kicked her out?" Ray asked.

The sympathy came back as quickly as it had left. "No. She turned sixteen. Our agreement with the county is that we keep them until they finish high school or turn sixteen. She dropped outta school in June as soon as the term ended, so we had to turn her out.

"I tried to talk her out of dropping out. I talked to her, Rachael talked to her, people at the school talked to her. LeAnn wasn't havin' any of it. Said she just wanted to get away and have her own life."

"How'd she end up with Mac and Ernestine?" Ray asked.

"I called them and asked if they'd put her up. Oh, I told them the whole story. Gave them fair warning what they could expect, which, if you ask me, was a pain in the neck, but they said to send her over. They were fine people, Ray. I truly hope LeAnn didn't do this, but if she did, I hope she pays dearly for it. They didn't deserve that."

"When did she move in with them?"

"That'd be early June. I can give you the exact date if you want it." He leafed rapidly through the file.

"No, that's okay," Ray offered.

"June sixth. I was gonna take her, but by the time I got back from Perry—I was getting parts for the truck—her boyfriend had already picked her up and taken her over there."

"She cause any trouble for the Martins? That you know of?"

"Well, I'd say it's a sure bet. Poor thing, she was born into trouble and didn't know any other way. But they never said anything to me about it."

Ray screwed up his face. "Never a word?"

"See, it's like this, Ray. Some men are more susceptible to sexual temptations than others." He looked at me and raised his eyebrows as if he expected a confirmation.

God, if only he knew to whom he was speaking, I thought. You ain't a-kiddin' some men are more susceptible! I nodded my head knowingly.

He went on: "Men like McHenry Martin, you, me, we got good solid families. Attractive women who love us and care about us at home. We got no need to be messin' around with sixteen-year-old whores. Other men aren't so lucky." He looked at me, and I nodded my head enthusiastically.

"That's why I figured it'd work with Mac and Ernie. Them being such good folks and all and knowing beforehand what kinda stuff LeAnn was liable to pull, well, I just figured she'd be safe with them."

"I never figured they might not be safe with her."

"Mm" was all Ray said. He stood up, and I followed suit. "I'll need to keep the pictures for the sheriff," he said as we started for the door.

"Sure. No problem. I got others," Jerry said, following us out. "Good luck finding her. I really hope she didn't have anything to do with this, Ray. You call me if there's anything else I can do, ya hear?"

"Yeah," Ray said as we made our way to the stairs

and started down. Then he turned suddenly and called back to the office. "Hey, Jerry?"

Jerry's head popped out through the doorway.

"Jerry, what's her boyfriend's name?"

"Adam Taylor. Lives over on Clark Mountain, I think," Jerry said.

"Yeah, I know where he lives," Ray said, shaking his head. "Shit," he mumbled.

Ray was quiet as we walked over to the boys' dormitory. He played with the cigarette for a bit longer, stuck it in his mouth, and then threw it away. He stopped and looked at me.

"You buy all of that?" he asked.

"Uh, yeah. I guess." Why wouldn't I? I had no reason to disbelieve Jerry Sites. I liked his handshake, and I liked him. He seemed to have that rare combination of enthusiasm and realism that so few ministers manage to create in their lives. "Shouldn't I?"

Ray held up the picture of the girl. She seemed more attractive in the moonlight. There was a strength in that face. Not pretty. Nothing like pretty. Strong, challenging, and confident and still feminine, almost pretty. You got the feeling that, if she decided to, she could kick your ass and make you like it.

"Could you refuse that if it was offered to you on a silver platter?"

Of all the people to ask! What should I say? I decided on the truth. "I don't know, Ray. I guess it would depend on how I felt at the moment. Saying no wouldn't be easy."

He put the picture in his pocket. "Bullshit! You'd be in it up to your belly button same as any man would. You're a man of God. How can you stand there and lie like that?"

"For God's sake, Ray, she's a kid. She's only sixteen years old."

"And she looks twenty-one, and your dick don't got eyes and it can't count. You think he was fuckin' her?"

Now it was my turn to stop. "Jeez, Ray! How should I know? What about his wife? He said she's attractive. Why would he want to mess around with something strange?"

"Because it's there. Just like those mountain climbers say. And let me tell you something about Mrs. Rachael Carter Sites. She's got red hair down to here that she must spend about twenty hours a day fixing up. She's got a figure that could stop traffic twenty miles away, and she don't mind men lookin' at her, either."

"Well, there you go, then," I said. Ray had just given a very good reason for Jerry Sites not screwing around with a sixteen-year-old tramp.

"And," he went on, "she got saved at a revival meeting about three years ago. Born-again, speakin'-in-tongues, baptism of the Holy Ghost, anti-everything *saved*!"

"That doesn't mean anything," I argued. "Some of the sexiest people I know are born-again Christians."

"Sexy she is. Sexual she ain't."

He pronounced it "sex-you-all," with the emphasis on "all."

"You don't know that."

"Mm" was all he said, and we started off toward the dorm again.

"Besides, even if he was sleeping with the girl, and

I don't think he was, what does that have to do with the Martins' fire?" I asked.

"Nothin'," he said. "Just interesting is all."

"You don't like Jerry Sites, do you?"

"You mean the Reverend Dr. Gerald Sites? Why wouldn't I like him?" he asked, innocent as the day he was born.

"I don't know, just the way you talk about him."

"He's a jerk. You see the way he dresses? That haircut? Who the hell's he tryin' to impress?"

"So he's a jerk who can't give up his big-city ways. That doesn't make him a child molester," I said.

He patted his pocket with the picture in it. "I don't think making it with this girl would be considered child molesting. Putting your balls in severe jeopardy, maybe, but not child molesting." He chuckled at his own humor.

"So what do you do now?" I asked.

"Well, first I help you get some furniture over to your house. Then I go home and take another shower and drink a coupla Buds. Then I watch 'L.A. Law' on the tube. Then, if I'm lucky, me and May June play a little tickle-butt before we get a good night's sleep. If I'm not lucky, I go to bed and fantasize about Rachael Sites and LeAnn Bertke ganging up on me. Damn if all this talk about screwing hasn't given me a case o' the hornies."

"I meant what do you do about the murders?" I said.

"First thing tomorrow morning I call Mr. William B. Fine, sheriff of Durel County and my second cousin, and I give him everything I got, and it becomes his problem."

"You mean you just walk away from it?"

"Yep. I'm a constable. I get a badge and two hundred dollars a month to clean up car wrecks and keep the moonshiners and pot growers under control. If I want a handgun I gotta buy it myself, so I don't want one. Most big crimes go to my cousin. That's the way he wants it, and that's fine with me."

By this time we were standing in one of the unused lounges of the boys' dorm. Ray had been walking around piling chairs, pillows, rugs, and everything else that wasn't nailed down onto a big threadbare overstuffed sofa. He bent down at one end and looked up at me.

"You gonna help, or you expect me to carry the whole thing?"

Exhaustion.

Utter, complete, mind-numbing, body-wrenching exhaustion.

It took us four trips to carry all of the stuff down to the parsonage from the boys' dorm, and we just dumped it in the little living room. I was too tired to try to do anything with it. By the time I thanked Ray and bid him farewell at my front door it was after 11:00 P.M., and I fell onto the couch in a daze.

In one day I had made the arduous journey from Louisville to Baird, had my first glimpse of my new church, moved into the parsonage, learned that two of my parishioners had been murdered and their house burned down, and met two guys who were probably the most prominent men in the small community. But exhausted as I was, sleep would not come. It was all too much. My mind wouldn't let go of it long enough for the gentle fog of sleep to penetrate.

I longed for a shot of Black Jack but would not,

could not, have drunk it even if I'd had it in the house. Since the big crash I had not allowed myself more than an occasional beer. Besides, the fridge was as empty as the surface of the moon, as were the cabinets and the larder.

So I packed my pipe, fetched a glass of tap water from the kitchen, turned on the radio to a "lite rock" station in Lexington, and let my mind wander.

Tomorrow would be Friday, which meant I had to put in some time on my first sermon in two years. This was not as much work as preachers lead us to believe. Basically I use the free-association method for writing sermons.

I pick a text early in the week. I read it several times, write it out, and put it in a prominent place—on my desk or, in this case, on the sun visor in the VW— and I think about it. You'd be surprised how much stuff happens in a week that is applicable to any given text. As stuff happens and ideas and stories become clear, I jot them down and fasten them to the text. Then, late in the week, I do some study in the commentaries and journals and make decisions about which stories and ideas don't really work. Those I throw away. What is left is the sermon.

It works better than it sounds. My parishioners may not have liked my moral character, but they have always loved my sermons.

Anyway, sometimes on Friday or Saturday I'd need to hit the books for a couple of hours. Right now they were still in a box in the backseat of the Vee-Dub.

McHenry and Ernestine Martin had been members of my church, which meant I'd have to bury them. On the way back from the fire, Ray had told me that they had had no relatives that he knew of, which meant a small service. I'd have to find out from the coroner's office in Perry which funeral home they'd been sent to and what arrangements had been made to find family. After that, the funeral would have to be planned. Probably on Monday, maybe Tuesday if distant relatives were found who had to travel a long way.

Then there was all the stuff that comes with starting a new position as a pastor. There would probably be a reception of some kind on Sunday afternoon, and, no doubt, two or three factions would compete to take me to lunch so they could tell me how wonderful or awful—depending on the faction—my predecessor had been.

I would also want to court some people myself. Jerry Sites seemed like a likely candidate. He was a fish out of water, like me, though he'd been out of his water longer than I had been out of mine. Still, the city never quite wears off a person, and Jerry wore his city manners like a suit of armor.

And while I was on the subject of Jerry Sites, what was Ray's problem with him, anyway? I did not believe for a minute that the Baptist minister and administrator was sleeping with LeAnn Bertke, his sixteen-year-old charge. Horny is horny, but stupid is stupid. Sleeping with a sixteen-year-old kid gets you more than thrown out of your church. It gets you thrown into the pokey! Jerry might be many things—affected, arrogant, citified—but he did not seem to be stupid.

Still, you had to wonder. Maybe it was a personality clash. Two strong, independent, influential men bashing heads. Baird was a pretty small pond, and it couldn't handle too many big fish.

And speaking of Ray, why was he so upset when Jerry mentioned LeAnn's boyfriend? He'd said he knew where the kid lived. Then he'd said, "Shit," sort of under his breath. What was that all about?

And copperheads. Christ, no one had said anything about snakes when discussing the possibility of sending me to Appalachia. And now they had them under the house at the Mountain Baptist Children's Home just across the road from me, and hadn't the Carmack twins said it was just about impossible to get them out from under a house? What about this house? Had anyone checked under it lately, I wondered?

The pipe was burning low, the water had gone warm, and I was too tired to continue. Free association was becoming free hallucination.

I called Mom, told her absolutely nothing of what I had really experienced that day, said everything was wonderful, hung up the phone, and fell sound asleep on the couch, comfortable in the knowledge that I'd not given my mother something to worry about.

Her last words to me before I hung up the phone were "I'm sure you'll do a fine job for those folks, Daniel. Just don't screw this one up. You do and you'll be dead in the water."

Mom. You gotta love her.

By seven o'clock Friday morning the temperature was close to eighty degrees and my neck was so stiff from sleeping on the couch that I had to get up. I took a cool shower, slipped into some cotton pants and a knit T-shirt, and, since the fridge was still empty, I walked over to the Baird Diner for breakfast.

May June poured me a cup of coffee as soon as I walked in the door, and I asked for a large glass of orange juice, which she poured from a carton. Before I could decline, she produced three over-easy eggs, six strips of bacon, a huge mountain of hash browns, and two buttermilk biscuits. Ah, well, it had been a hard night. I'd worry about cholesterol tomorrow.

"Where's the lord of the manor?" I asked, as I sopped up the last of the egg yolk with a piece of biscuit.

May June refilled my coffee cup. "On the phone," she said. "Talking to that worthless cousin of his in Perry."

"Sheriff Fine?"

"Fine for nothin'," she said, slapping at a fly with a dish towel.

It was too early to hear about worthless relatives, a complaint which, I have found, knows no geo-ethnic-political boundaries, so I tried to change the subject.

"I met Reverend Sites last night. Seems like a nice fellow," I ventured.

"He's a fine man. I wish he and Ray got along better."

"Ray and him don't see eye to eye," I said, trying to be helpful and hoping to get more of the story.

"Oh, nothin' like fighting or anything. They just kinda circle each other all the time like a couple of gamecocks that's too old to fight and too proud not to." She picked up my dishes. "You done with these?"

I patted my stomach and nodded. "Delicious. Ray and Jerry get into it over something?"

"Never a thing," she said. "They're too civilized for that. I just think they don't like each other. Ray thinks Reverend Sites's a peacock, and the reverend, he thinks Ray's an ignorant redneck. 'Course, they'd never say it out loud, but that's what they both think."

"Mm." Culture clash. It was odd but not unheard of. People from different cultures don't understand each other, so they don't like each other. Simple and sad. Together the two of them might do a lot for Baird. But it probably wouldn't happen because they were both too proud and too headstrong to back away and admit that the other had something to offer.

While I was polishing off my third cup of coffee, Ray came out of the constable's office swearing and growling like a black bear.

"Worthless little son of a bitch. I shoulda killed him when he was a kid. What am I supposed to do now?" He walked behind the plywood counter and poured himself a mug of coffee as big as a beer stein.

May June winked at me. "His cousin. He really loves that boy. He's just too macho to let anyone see it."

"Bullshit," Ray grumbled. "The little shit wouldn't know a murder if happened to him in his own house. Stupid little fuck. I shoulda just let him drown that time at Viper Quarry. Save the whole damn county from him."

Ray looked at me and saw from my expression, I suppose, that I didn't know what he was talking about.

"When we were kids we used to go swimmin' over to Viper in the quarry pits. 'Bout a thousand feet deep and cold as a well digger's butt. Billy's about eight years younger'n me, but he begged to go along. Dove into the only shallow place in the whole damn pit and busted his head. I hauled him out and took him to Perry and got him sewed up." Ray drank two gulps from his steaming coffee mug. The stuff would have scalded a lesser man, I thought.

"Anyway," he went on. "Now he's got this notion that I saved his life and so in gratitude he appoints me constable of Baird Township. Big fuckin' deal. Two hundred dollars a month and a thousand pages of paperwork. Cheap little fuck don't even supply me with my own gun. I want one I gotta buy it myself."

"Which you aren't gonna do," May June said.

"Which I'm not gonna do, Mother. Don't worry."

"So what'd he say about the Martin murders?" I asked.

"Fuck him!" Ray yelled and slammed his fist down on the counter. "The stupid little shit says from where he stands it looks more like a house fire and a runaway. God damn!"

"From where he stands?"

"Yeah. And I'll tell you where he stands. With his nose planted firmly up the ass of the mayor of Perry, that's where. The boy has forgot where he come from. He's forgot his roots. All the little shit kicker cares about is gettin' elected again. He don't give two shits about some redneck hillbilly family gettin' killed in the mountains." He drained the coffee, started to get some more, changed his mind, and got a Bud from one of the refrigerators. He held one up to me.

I shook my head. "Too early for me."

"Well, it ain't over, by God," he said, popping the top on the Bud and taking a healthy gulp. "I'm the law in Baird Township, and it ain't over till I say it's over. Mac Martin was good people, and I'm gonna find the fucker that did this to him, I swear to God."

"Well, then, you better get started," May June said, wiping the counter. "You'll feel better when you're doin' something. Where you gonna start?"

Ray drained the beer can, crushed it, and threw it in a trash can under the counter while he thought. "First thing we gotta do is find that girl," he said.

"You don't think that was her in the bed at the

house?" I asked. "Maybe Ernestine came home and found Mac and LeAnn in the sack and, uh, done 'em in?"

They both looked at me as though I'd just dropped my pants in a public place.

"Why, that's the most ridiculous thing I've ever heard," May June said, clucking her tongue. "Shame on you for thinking such a thing."

"I just thought . . ."

"Well, stop thinking it. There's no way in this world or any other that McHenry Martin would be unfaithful to his wife. He was a Christian and a leader in his church."

I wanted to tell her that those things didn't amount to a dandelion seed in a whirlwind when it came to sex. I oughta know. But I kept my peace because Ray was giving me a look that could have melted an anvil. Besides, I wanted to put my past behind me, not bring it up every time it illustrated my side of an argument.

"Well, let's go, then," Ray said to me, coming around the counter and heading for the door.

"Where are we going?" I asked.

"We're gonna find that girl," he said, holding the screen door open.

"We? Hey, wait a minute. I have to write a sermon. I've got ten tons of furniture sitting in my living room, and I have to prepare a funeral service for the Martins. I'm the new preacher in town, remember?"

"Yeah, well, now you're a deputy constable. Ain't no way I'm goin' up to Clark Mountain alone." He fanned the screen door to keep the flies out. "Come on."

"There's no such thing as a deputy constable. A

constable *is* a deputy"—I turned to May June—"isn't it?"

She shrugged her shoulders and smiled. "I'm just the cook."

"What about my furniture? I don't have any food in the house. What am I supposed to eat?" I asked, frantically trying to find a way out of this thing.

Ray grumbled and let the door slam shut. "Jesus. You can eat with us. Mother, close the store this afternoon and get some of the ladies to help you set up the new preacher's house for him."

"No need to close the store," she said. "I'll get Darnell to watch things. But what am I gonna tell the girls? That our new pastor's out investigating a murder?"

"Tell 'em I'm introducin' him around the community," Ray said. Then to me, "Will you come on?"

We climbed into his jeep and he shot out onto Route 42 at his usual breakneck speed. I searched for a seat belt, found none, and contented myself with holding on as best I could to the roll bar and the dashboard. We had to scream at each other to carry on a conversation.

"Didn't want you to upset May June," Ray shouted. "She thought the world of Mac and Ernie. And she's a good Christian woman but a little delicate, if you know what I mean."

I thought I had seen bulldozers more delicate than May June Hall. She was maybe five-four or five-five and probably went about two hundred pounds. She had biceps as big as Ray's, and her frumpy housedresses didn't hide her sure, confident, capable assertiveness. At least it wasn't hidden from me. But then, I wasn't married to her.

"I just thought it was something worth considering," I said.

"I already considered it," he said, crinkling an eye at me. "The body in the bedroom wasn't more than five feet tall—Ernestine's size. This LeAnn's five feet seven inches tall."

"How d'you know that?"

"It was in the file that the Reverend Dr. Sites was trying to keep me from seein' last night. I caught a glimpse when we got up to leave."

Ray Hall was a bundle of surprises. Constable, postmaster, merchant, and sleuth. Sort of an Appalachian version of a Renaissance man. I wondered what else he could do.

"So where are we going now?" I screamed over the wind and the Jeep's abused muffler.

"Clark Mountain. Gonna talk with that boyfriend of LeAnn's. That's why I wanted you to come along."

"Why is that?"

"He's a Taylor. They hate me."

"Oh," I said, nodding as though it was the most normal thing in the world. Of course! They hate you. Why else would you want someone to go with you? You go to talk to someone who hates you, you take a new preacher from the city with you.

Wonderful.

I don't know what I expected to find at the top of Clark Mountain. . . .

Okay, I guess I really do know what I expected to find. What I expected to find was either the Hatfields or the McCoys. I expected to find a group of poor, weathered hillbillies dressed in bib overalls. I pictured them with beards down to here, sweat-stained floppy hats, wheat stalks in their mouths, and muskets hanging over their arms. I expected them to have earthenware jugs on the porch with three X's on them.

I expected their women to be barefoot, pregnant, ignorant, downtrodden, and pitiful.

I expected to see a coonhound lying under the porch and a pump in the front yard.

There was a coonhound, but he was sitting under a dune buggy with tires at least two feet wide. That was about as far as my expectations got me.

The house was a big two-story Colonial that couldn't have been more than ten or twelve years old.

70

Used brick, big columns in front, broad porch with nearly new patio furniture on it. The yard was pure Kentucky bluegrass and looked as if it had been manicured with barber shears and a comb.

Besides the dune buggy, there was a new Ford Bronco, a Ford pickup truck that was a couple of years old, an old Ford Falcon in mint condition, and a big old LTD starting to rust around the rocker panels. A Ford family, I guess you could say.

But more surprising than any of this was the women—or woman, I should say—who greeted us. Nothing of the poor, ignorant, pregnant hillbilly here.

She was maybe twenty-five years old. Five feet six or so with a ripe but firm figure. Big round breasts and tight well-muscled hips, all of which was well displayed beneath a plain white T-shirt and a pair of jeans that were cut off so that they formed a *V* at the crotch, the pockets hanging out from beneath the frayed legs of the shorts.

Her hair was dark and pulled back into what my ex-wife used to call a George-type ponytail. Her eyes were such a bright blue that they nearly shone, and her mouth was broad with full pink lips.

And the most arresting thing of all—the thing I found almost unbearably erotic about her—was her shoes. Air Jordans with sweat socks bagging down over the tops.

Don't try to figure it out. I was in love.

She came to the front door of the house as we pulled into the yard, bounded over to the side of the Jeep, smiled, and said, "Hey, Ray!"

"Hey, Naomi. How you doin', darlin'?"

She looked at me but kept talking to Ray. All I

could think of was what the Jeep ride must have done to my hair.

"I'm fine, Ray. Just fine. How're you?"

"Just fine."

"Miz Hall?"

"She's fine, too."

"How's Darnell doin'?"

Now Ray was watching her watching me. I think she knew how uncomfortable I was, and he knew that she knew. And I knew that he knew that she knew. And all of this knowing wasn't doing me a bit of good, because I was still as uncomfortable as I could be. I kept trying to look everywhere but at Naomi, but my eyes wouldn't obey my brain.

"Darnell's fine, too," Ray said. "Your daddy?"

She shrugged. "Oh, you know Daddy."

He nodded. "I reckon I do."

"Who's this here?" she asked, flipping her head toward me, not breaking her gaze.

"Oh, this here's the new Methodist preacher," Ray said, as though he'd forgotten I was sitting there. Good old Ray, always the comedian. "Name's Reverend Thompson. Daniel or Dan but not Danny or Dano."

She let her gaze scrutinize my entire body, up and down. I knew how women must feel when men did it to them, and beauty or not she was beginning to piss me off a little. Teasing I can take, but I got the feeling she was trying to humiliate me, using her obvious sexuality as a weapon.

Finally, mercifully, she looked away from me to Ray. "He don't look like a preacher," she said.

"Oh, he's a preacher, all right."

"He don't dress like a preacher."

"Ordained and everything," Ray said, winking at me. "And, Naomi, he ain't married, either."

Now she was the one to be embarrassed. She slapped at Ray's big shoulder and stood up straight. "Oh, Ray. Now, what would I care if he's married or not?"

"Well, I just figured you'd like to know. Girl your age ought to think about getting married. Don't want that body to go to waste." Now he was grinning broadly, enjoying her embarrassment. She was getting as good as she gave, and Ray had been in the middle of both exchanges. He seemed to have found his element.

"Ray," she said, exasperated, "he's a preacher!"

And there it was.

Despite the fact that my great crash came as a result of a sexual indiscretion, let me set the record straight on something right now. Most women, if they find a minister attractive, do so only from afar. As a rule, we tend to have a certain ego strength, charisma, charm, and character that some women admire. From afar!

But if a woman includes those things in her mental image of a minister, she will also, no doubt, include things like morally correct, stalwart, rigid, naive, pure, and virginal.

So there you have it: passionate but sexless, driven but not ambitious, moral but not judgmental, powerful but weak, smart but not cunning, educated but naive, wise but innocent. That's how women, and many men, see ministers.

You doubt it? Okay, try to imagine your own minister naked. Or having sex. Or passing gas. Or belching. Or taking a pee.

73

See? We all do those things, but no one wants to admit it or even think about it.

So is it any wonder that women are at once attracted to us and repelled by us? No, it is to be expected.

And that morning, sitting in Ray's Jeep, that expectation, realized, was breaking my heart.

Naomi leaned over Ray and, quite properly, offered me her hand. "Pleased to meet you, Reverend Dan," she said.

I shook her hand and managed somehow to control an urge to yank her into the Jeep and make passionate love to her. "Just Dan is fine, Miss Taylor," I said.

"I'm taking him around, introducing him to all the folks in the area," Ray said, by way of explaining my presence.

"Are you folks Methodists?" I asked her, refusing to relinquish my hold on her hand.

She started to pull it back, but stopped. "Well, I guess not," she said. "We used to be Baptists, but we don't go to church much anymore. Just for—"

"Marrying and burying," we said together.

She laughed, and I thought my heart would melt and run through the hole in the floorboard of the Jeep.

"Well," Ray said, rousing us from our reverie. "I guess I oughta find your daddy and introduce him to the new preacher."

Naomi let go of my hand and stood up straight again. She was starting to perspire, standing there in the sun, and the T-shirt seemed to be getting thinner. "He's 'round back in the garden," she said to Ray. "Go on around and I'll bring you all a beer." Then, to me: "Lemonade be okay, Rev . . . uh, Dan?"

"A beer would be just as good," I said.

"Oh," she said, a little surprise in her voice. Then a small smile. "Okay. Budweiser okay?"

"Whatever's cold," I said.

She smiled and went off toward the house. I watched her walk most of the way and noticed Ray watching her, too. When she was in the house and we were climbing out of the Jeep, I said to Ray, "I thought the Taylors hated you."

"The menfolk do," he said.

"But not Naomi."

"No. Not Naomi. She's special, that one."

"Tell me about it," I said, sighing.

"And she's twenty years younger than you," Ray said sternly. "And her daddy's the meanest man this side of hell."

"Well . . ."

"Well, nothin'," he said. "Just put it far from your mind . . . Preacher."

My mother has a garden. It's about eight feet by sixteen feet. Landscaping timbers stacked two high on all four sides and full of mulch and well-seasoned topsoil. She grows tomatoes and peppers and flowers. Some onions, maybe, and a head or two of cabbage just for fun.

That's what I think of when I think of a garden.

Hebrew Taylor had something more on the order of a small farm in his backyard. Two acres, easy. Sweet corn, three kinds of tomatoes that I could see, peppers green and red, acorn squash, string beans, cabbage, lettuce, radishes, carrots, several things I couldn't identify, and, of course, tobacco.

I'd never seen a garden so big or so well tended. There was not a weed in sight. It would have been an obscenity in such a beautiful, well-tended work of art.

The earth was rich and black against the red clay that surrounded it, and the whole thing was well hoed, loose, and finely chopped.

The patriarch of the Taylor clan stood in the middle of it all, tall and thin, silver hair, deeply tanned, wearing a pair of blue jeans that had lost all of their color and a long-sleeved cotton plaid shirt buttoned up to his throat. He wasn't doing anything. Just standing with a hoe in his hand and looking down and across the garden.

We stood at the edge for a moment, and at length, Ray cleared his throat and started to speak. "Uh, excuse me, there, Hebe . . ."

The old man held up his hand for silence, and Ray stopped. We watched as he ducked his head slightly and stared intently at the ground toward the string beans about three rows over from where he stood. He lifted his foot slowly and took a step, then another, and then began a sort of weird, hopping walk into the beans as though he was stalking something.

"What's he doing?" I whispered to Ray.

Ray shrugged. "Beats the hell outta me."

We continued to watch the performance for a few more minutes; then the old man suddenly threw his hoe at the ground, swore, and began a mad dash toward our side of the garden.

"Son of a bitch! Get 'im! Get 'im, dammit. Don't just stand there!"

Ray and I looked down the edge of the garden, and Ray realized, just before I did, that Taylor was chasing something out of the vegetables. We made a dash for the spot where it was presumably headed and stood there, waiting.

"You see 'im?" shouted Taylor.

"What am I lookin' for, Hebe?" Ray yelled.

"Christ! you're lookin' for Tut. He just took off that way . . ."

"Oh, shit," Ray said under his breath.

". . . and he's gonna get out if we don't get 'im. You see 'im?"

"No, Hebe, I don't."

"Wait!" Taylor threw up his arm and froze. "I got 'im."

Again he went into slow motion, one hand outstretched for balance, the other reaching out in front of him, ready to make a grab.

I was at a complete loss. "Ray," I whispered again, "who's Tut?"

"Oh, it's that goddamn—"

"Got 'im!" cried Taylor from somewhere close by in the garden. He was completely out of sight now, crawling around on the ground among the string beans. Then he popped up about ten feet in front of us. He was holding a huge black and yellow snake.

"Jesus!" I said, jumping back and tripping over a lawn chair that had been set up facing the garden. I caught my balance just before I went down and braced myself on the chair. "I thought you were chasing a dog."

"Nah, just ol' Tut, here," Taylor said, smiling. The snake was wrapping itself around his arm, and it looked to be just over five feet long and about as big around as the old man's wrist. He held it about ten inches back from the head, but it made no move to turn or bite him.

"Tut?" I could feel my legs getting weak.

"Yessir. King Tut. Best ratter in the county. Good

for copperheads and rattlers, too. But he's got a wan-
derin' eye. He takes off every chance he gets."

A can of Budweiser appeared in front of my face
as I sank into the lawn chair.

"He's a king snake," Naomi Taylor said. "They're
good guys. They feed on rodents and other snakes,
and they're immune to the venom."

I took the beer and drank half of it in one swig.
"Does he know that we're good guys, too?"

"Sure," she said. She handed another beer to Ray
and a third to her father, who handed the big serpent
to her. The snake immediately began to wrap itself
around her arm. "They actually seem to like humans
and enjoy being held as long as you let them support
their weight by wrapping themselves around you." She
switched the snake's head to her left hand and used
her right to help the snake coil itself around her shoulders. "If I just let him hang from my hand, his own
weight would snap his spine." She held the thing out
to me. "Wanna hold him?"

I shrunk back. "Maybe later. When we've been
properly introduced."

"You got rats in your garden, Hebe?" Ray asked.

The old man's face had been, up to now, happy and
filled with what looked like pride—in his daughter or
in his pet, I couldn't tell—but at the sound of Ray's
voice, his expression changed immediately into something more like disgust. Maybe even anger.

"No. Hell, no, I ain't got rats in my garden, Constable." He said it as though he were saying something
obscene.

Ray didn't rise to the bait. He just waited.

'What I got's copperheads. Seen two this morning

when I was doing my morning hoeing. So I let Tut in here to see if he could sniff 'em out."

"Do any good?" Ray asked.

"Does it look like he done any good?" Exasperation now mixed with the answer. "He took off for greener pastures just as soon as I let him down. Stupid thing's gettin' old and cussed."

"Just like someone else I know," Naomi said, winking at me.

"Just watch your mouth, young lady," the old man said, still mad. "You just watch your mouth and remember where you are."

Her smile disappeared, but there was still something of a grin in her eyes.

Ray seemed embarrassed by the old man's outburst. "This here's the new Methodist preacher, Hebe. Name's Dan Thompson." He pointed at me, and I stood and started to extend my hand, but the old man turned and walked back to the center of the garden.

"Don't go into churches," he said, picking up his hoe.

"I don't go into coal mines," I said. "But I still need the coal to keep my house warm in the winter."

"What the hell is that supposed to mean?" Taylor said, walking toward us. "That some kind o' smart-ass city-preacher put-down? Think you can smart-talk us hicks into coming to your church? Show us how clever you are?"

Whoa! Pretty hostile. I decided to backwater a little. "I'm sorry, Mr. Taylor. I didn't mean any disrespect. I was just trying to—"

"Get me to come to that church o' yours and cough up enough money to fix the furnace or some damn thing. I know what you were trying to do. But you can forget it. Me and the Lord do all our talking right here." He sat down heavily in the chair. As robust as he looked, he must have been nearly sixty, and the heat and activity seemed to have taken a heavy toll on him.

I looked at Naomi, and she rolled her eyes and readjusted the snake, which was now curled around her shoulders. It's not you, she seemed to be saying. He's like this with everyone.

"I wonder if you can tell me where Adam is," Ray said to the old man.

"Why? You gonna bust him like you did Josh and Jake on some trumped-up drug charge?" He drank some of his beer and wiped his chin with his sleeve.

Ray sighed. "No, Hebe. I just wanna talk to him. Seems he was seeing this girl from the children's home, and we're having some trouble locating her."

"Her! Little white-trash slut's all she is. I run her off."

"You ran her off? When was this?"

"I don't remember. Couple of days ago. Come flouncing herself around here like a bitch in heat, and I run her off. Told Adam she was trouble and he should stay away from her."

"Where'd she go?"

"Don't know."

"What about Adam?"

"What about him?" Taylor seemed to be having trouble breathing. He was sucking in small gasps of air, and his color seemed to be getting gray.

"How'd he feel about you running the girl off?" Ray asked.

"He did like I told him. He forgot about her. And

a good thing, too. Little white-trash slut. Crazy as her daddy, you ask me."

"How do you know she was crazy?" Ray asked.

The old man turned and looked at Ray and sighed. "Well, fer chrissake, her old man was crazy as a hoot owl, wasn't he? Well, the apple don't fall far from the tree, does it?"

"She do anything crazy? Threaten you or your family or anything?"

"Hell, no. She just turned on her round little heel and flounced out's what she done. And a good thing, too, or I'da sicced the dog on her."

"What about Adam?" Ray asked again.

"I done told you, he done like he was told." The old man was gasping now, sucking breath like an asthmatic.

"Can I talk to him?"

"No need. I told you all you need to know."

"Still, I need to—"

"Naomi!"

Naomi jumped and ran toward the house. "I'll get your bottle, Daddy," she yelled over her shoulder.

Ray watched her go to the house. "I'd still like to talk to your boy, Hebe. Just to see if he has any idea . . ."

"You leave my boy alone!"

". . . where she might have gone off to."

"He don't know nothing."

Ray didn't add anything. He just stood there, looking at the old man, who was gasping, fighting for breath.

Naomi came running out of the house with a little oxygen bottle and fit the mask over the old man's face. She turned the valve, and Taylor's chest expanded and his color began to return almost immediately.

Naomi turned to Ray and sighed. "Adam's working at the mine today. He's driving one of the trucks, I think. You'll have to catch him on the road or between trips."

Ray nodded. "Thanks, Naomi." His gaze drifted to the old man as he spoke. "I'm sorry."

"Yeah," she said. "I know."

Coal.

It is both life and death to Appalachia.

When demand is low, life is tough. The winters are cold, the cars get repossessed, mortgage payments go unpaid.

But when demand is high. Ah, then life is sweet indeed. Nice houses, pickup trucks with those big crew cabs, satellite dishes, microwave ovens.

Black lung.

Even as it gives us life, it gives us death.

Coal dust slowly turns lungs to stone, and strong men grow weak as they drown in their own phlegm. It is a slow, painful, terrible way to die. Torture.

It was killing Hebrew Taylor.

As we flew along the Baird-Towne Road toward Towne and the Clark Mine, dodging coal trucks and potholes, Ray Hall spit, swore, and spoke of it in intimate terms.

"Christ, I hated it. I only spent three years in the

mines, and I still wake up coughing every morning. I spit up stuff that makes me gag if I look at it."

"You worked for Mr. Taylor?" I yelled over the noise of the Jeep.

"Naw, I worked for a union mine over on Mount Devoux. Three years till I got a stake, and I was out. Bought the store and never went near a mine again." He hawked and spit as though the mere thought of it brought up phlegm.

"Is that why Mr. Taylor doesn't like you? Because you quit?" I asked.

"Nope. That's why he tolerates me at all. He knows I got good sense. He hates me on accounta what I done to his boys. I caught the eldest two, Josh and Jake, peddling cocaine. I ran 'em in to the sheriff's office, and they both done a year in the state prison."

"Just a year?" I was remembering that a similar offense in Louisville's inner city would win you a fifteen-year scholarship.

"They copped a plea to simple possession, and their daddy pulled some strings for 'em." Ray didn't seem upset or bitter about it.

"Hebrew Taylor must have a lot of muscle in this county," I ventured.

"Plenty. He owns this whole mountain, everything under it, in it, and on it. Timber, coal, minerals, water, everything. He's one rich old fart." Ray spit again. "You see the size of that house? The satellite dish? The cars?"

I agreed that it was all impressive. "He's come pretty far for a lowly coal miner. How'd he do it?"

"He didn't do it. His granddaddy done it. His granddaddy was the Clark this mountain's named for. Clark Taylor. His only son was Hebrew's daddy. Hebe was his daddy's only son." He raised an eyebrow at me as if to ask, You got all that?

"So how did he get black lung if he was a poor little rich boy?" I asked, indicating that I had indeed gotten all the story.

"He got black lung 'cause his daddy was a prick," Ray said. My face must have betrayed my confusion, so he continued. "Ol' Andrew said he wasn't gonna have his boy runnin' off to college. Said the only education his son needed to run the Clark Taylor Coal Concern was to be found at the bottom of a shaft. So that's where Hebrew went to get his education. Every dirty, stupid, dangerous job came along, Hebe done it. Went down when he was fourteen years old and came out when he was thirty-five, the day his daddy died. Ain't been back down since, as far as anybody knows. Won't let any of his boys go down in one even for a look around. 'Course, twenty-one years was long enough, I guess."

Twenty-one years at the bottom of a coal mine to learn an object lesson. "His father's to blame for his black lung disease, then, isn't he?" I asked. "Hebrew never really had to go down in the mines. His daddy killed him."

Ray spit again. "I reckon that's the way Hebe sees it, too," he said.

"That's why he was so touchy about my coal metaphor."

Ray looked at me and smiled. "You're learnin'," he said. "You wanna pop or something?"

We had pulled to a roaring stop in front of a little store in Towne, a burg that barely deserved its name. The store, a Phillips 66 station, and a post office were all that marked its presence.

I ordered a diet Pepsi and selected to stay in the Jeep and smoke my pipe, smoking having been an impossibility as we sped around the mountain. Ray must have known the proprietor; I could hear their voices in jovial greeting. I couldn't make out what they said, but the noise of conversation was clear.

Directly he emerged through the screen door, letting it slam behind him, and threw me a regular Pepsi, announcing that they didn't have diet anything and this would have to do. I have drunk diet soda for so long that I can scarcely stomach the sugared varieties, but I didn't say as much. I popped it and took a sip as Ray took a pull from his root beer and climbed into the Jeep.

"Well, either Naomi lied to us or Adam lied to her," he announced. "Adam ain't driving today."

Again my face gave me away.

"Aw, hell, Preacher, don't look so forlorn. Naomi ain't told a lie since she was a toddler. She ain't capable of it. She can tease, and she can give as good as she gets in a word fight, but she's honest as the day is long, and lyin' ain't in her nature. Adam probably lied to her." He started the engine and backed out onto the road. "But as long as we're up here we might as well just look and see for ourselves."

We started back up the mountain, and within fifteen minutes Ray made a skidding turn onto a gravel road that wound another thirty minutes up the mountain. The going was slower now, so the noise was not such a big problem. Dust, however, threatened to choke us both whenever we tried to talk.

"How do you know Adam isn't working today?" I asked, immediately clamping my handkerchief back over my mouth.

Ray didn't seem to notice the dust. "Old Harley James owns the Towne Store, back there. All the drivers come by it on their way to and from Perry with the coal, and they usually stop in for coffee in the morning on their way to the mine. He hasn't seen Adam or his truck all day."

The dust was beginning to make my eyes tear, and I coughed into my handkerchief, trying to clear it out of my throat. "Ray, we must have passed two dozen trucks since we left the Taylors' house. How can he be sure none of them was Adam?"

"Paint jobs," Ray said. He hawked and spit the dust out of his throat. "Damn! Those boys get paid tonnage bonuses, so they drive like hell and use the whole road until another car comes along. But they're real superstitious. They paint their truck cabs like those fighter-bomber crews did during World War Two. Won't let anyone else drive their trucks, either."

"Harley knows what Adam's truck looks like?"

"Yep. He says it's covered with flames just like those old hot rods used to be. Bet a dollar we'll find it sitting up at the mine."

And sure enough, there it was. A big black Mack dump truck with thin orange flames lapping up over the front grill. It sat in a gravel lot surrounded by pickups and cars. A hand-lettered sign where the road dumped into the lot said Clark Taylor Coal Concern—Mine No. 1.

"Hebrew Taylor's got more than one mine?" I asked as Ray cut the engine on the Jeep.

"Four," Ray answered. "But this is the onliest one he keeps going. He's non-union, so it's hard for him to keep an eye on more than one at a time. Besides, he's doing all right with this one."

We climbed from the Jeep, pounded the dust off of our clothes, and walked toward a house trailer at the end of the lot. Next to it was a toolshed, beyond which were the coal cars and tracks which, I presumed, led on down to the mouth of the mine itself. Another hand-lettered sign beside the door of the trailer said Kenneth Bogar, Superintendent. Ray entered without knocking.

Kenneth Bogar, superintendent of the Clark Mine No. 1, was a little banty rooster of a man with Italian features and Elvis hair and sideburns. He wore high-heeled cowboy boots, faded Levi's, and a white T-shirt that still had the fold marks from the store where it was bought. He made no secret of his dislike for Ray Hall.

"Whadaya want?" he asked, crushing out a cigarette in an overflowing tin ashtray.

"Now, Booger, is that any way to treat a duly appointed officer of the law?" Ray said, winking at me. Laughter danced behind his eyes.

Bogar's eyes hardened, and his face reddened at the intentional mispronunciation of his name, but he said nothing.

"I just came up here to introduce our new Methodist preacher," Ray went on. "Say hi to the Reverend Dr. Daniel Thompson from Louisville."

Bogar looked at me with much the same contempt he seemed to feel toward Ray. "Hi."

"There ya go," Ray said. "Adam Taylor workin' today?"

"No." Bogar leaned back and crossed his arms over his chest.

"Not at all?"

"You seen his truck out there. He ain't workin'."

"He come in this morning?" Ray began walking around the trailer, picking up things, inspecting them, and putting them back.

"How the hell should I know? You think I hold his hand just 'cause he's the boss's boy, you got another think ..."

Ray had stopped by the time clock near the front door and was going through the cards stacked next to it. He pulled one out, looked at it, and held it up.

Bogar sighed. "He might have been here this morning. He musta got sick and forgot to clock out."

"How you know he didn't clock out?" Ray asked, looking at the card. "You been sitting in here all morning watching that time clock?"

"No, Constable. I gotta work for a living. I don't just sit in here on my ass."

"Then how you know he didn't clock out?"

"I just allowed as how he didn't clock out 'cause—"

"And for that matter, how'd you know he clocked in, if he ain't working? Jesus, Bogar, you're a sorry liar, and that's a fact."

"Okay, goddamn it. He come in and then he took off with one of the boys. He's the boss's boy, for chrissake. What am I supposed to do, tattle on him? He wants to skin the old man, that's between them. He don't drive worth a shit anyhow."

"Reckless?"

"Christ, no! Too damn slow. Don't make more'n three, four trips a day. Too busy chasing tail to have his mind on work."

"Got his mind on the wrong bidness, Booger?" Ray laughed and winked at me again. "He been chasing any particular tail lately?"

"Now, how the hell should I know?" Bogar shook

another cigarette out of his pack of Pall Malls and lit it. Hadn't any of these people heard of filters? "I don't ask my drivers about their love lives."

"You seem to know about Adam's."

"It's just an expression. Chasing tail. You know."

"He never brought any up here?"

"Christ! Why would he do that?" Smoke billowed from Bogar's mouth and nose as he talked.

"Oh, you know how some of these drives are. They bring a girl up here, show 'em their truck, talk about how dangerous it is, driving so fast and all. Some of them boys figure their truck's the onliest thing bigger and more powerful than their pecker. Figure the girl'll think that, too." Ray was grinning from ear to ear, loving every minute of this

"Bullshit. You're just full of bullshit, you know that? Ain't no girl was ever impressed by a dump truck. Especially a girl like that little ..."

Ray looked up and smiled. "Like that little what?"

"That little tart Adam's been seein'."

"Then you've seen her? Around here?"

"No. Hell, I seen her in Perry last Saturday at the dance at the Am-Vets. Struttin' around like she's givin' it away's what she was doin'."

"This her?" Ray produced the school picture of LeAnn Bertke that Jerry Sites had given him.

"Yeah, I guess that's her. What's she done?"

"Nothing that I know of. I just need to talk to her's all."

Bogar's eyes lit up, and he grinned, showing crooked brown teeth. "Yeah, I bet that's what you wanna do. I wouldn't mind talking to her myself." The smile disappeared in a flash. "But I wouldn't mess with that. Underage pussy can fuck a man up bad. And that kind right there is the worst kind they is."

Ray put the picture back in his shirt pocket and took out his notebook and began writing. "What kind's that, Boog?"

"Loose kind's what kind," Bogar said. "She ain't no better'n a whore, with them skintight jeans and peekaboo shirts. No, sir, I stay clean away from that."

"You do that, Boog," Ray said, ripping a sheet from his notebook. "And if you see Adam, tell him to call me. I need to talk to him."

Bogar looked at the note. "Yeah, fat chance. The way his daddy feels about you."

Ray nodded at me, and we started out the door. "Just tell him, okay?"

"Yes, sir, Mr. Constable, sir. Will there be anything else, sir?" He said "Constable" as though it hurt his jaw to pronounce the word.

Ray stopped and leaned back in the door. "Yeah, Booger, there is one other little thing." Bogar threw his cigarette butt at the ashtray and sighed again. "Move your stash," Ray said. "Cut it in half. I don't mind a man growing a little weed for his own personal use any more'n I mind a man making up a little shine or home brew for his own kitchen. But when a man hides ten pounds of grass in an old milk box under the Sulfur Creek bridge I gotta figure he's selling more'n he's using. And you can ask the Taylor boys how I feel about drug peddlers in my township.

Ray closed the trailer door, and we walked toward the parking lot.

"He's selling dope?" I asked. "Booger's a dealer?"

Ray shook his head and chuckled. "No, hell. That's why he hates me so much. He thinks I put word out that I'd bust anyone who buys from him. Thing is, anyone wants grass around here grows their own. No need for a dealer." His chuckle began to turn into laugh. "An' old Booger, he's so dumb, he hides his stash in the same three places he's been hidin' it for the last two years and can't figure out how I know where it is."

As we got in the Jeep, Kenneth Bogar strutted across the parking lot and slapped a note onto the windshield of Adam Taylor's big dump truck. When he started back across the lot he saw us watching and threw his right fist into the air in front of his face, across and behind his left forearm—a classic Sicilian gesture of contempt.

Ray nearly fell out of the Jeep laughing.

here's something about a man's dirty underwear that is intensely personal. It's not something that you want a stranger, especially a woman, looking at. Often, in examining my own Jockey shorts, I wonder why my mother never seemed to have that same compulsion of so many mothers to see to it that her son died in spotless undies.

Oh, she kept mine clean when I was a kid. But she didn't go out of her way to keep them in good repair. If they held everything in place and kept it fairly well covered, that was all she cared about. The occasional stain or hole never seemed to give her a second thought.

My ex-wife had a similar attitude. Nothing so intentionally negligent as Mom's, but the result was usually the same. She seemed to think that a wash, a rinse, and a toss in the dryer defined the parameters of her responsibilities. If they didn't come out perfect, that was my problem. And, of course, she was right. Replacing my own worn underwear was my responsibility.

Having been so profoundly influenced by the two primary women in my life and their lack of concern for the care of my foundational garments, you can no doubt understand that such care did not find itself in a very exalted position on my own list of priorities.

So I was a little shocked and a little embarrassed to find, upon my arrival back at the parsonage, that May June Hall had unpacked my few boxes, washed my clothes from the night before, bleached them, dried them, pressed them, mended them, and left them folded neatly on my newly made up bed.

My once yellowed Jockey shorts were now blindingly white, fully mended, and folded neatly on the top of the stack. I paused for a minute, wondering what state they must have been in after I had driven all day in the hot VW and then tromped through the ashes of the Martin home, felt my face flush, and then let it go.

She must have seen worse, I figured. I hoped.

A fine thing. To see the seat of your pastor's dirty underwear before you hear his first sermon.

Which thought brought me to the little study between the parsonage and the church. This was what I had come home to do—to work on my sermon.

Ray and I had arrived back in Baird a little after noon, having taken nearly an hour to come back down Clark Mountain. Ray had invited me to go with him over to the Baird School to talk to some of LeAnn Bertke's school chums, but I had declined the invitation, insisting that I had to get unpacked, work on the sermon, find out when the funeral for the Martins would be, and drive into Perry for some groceries.

Now I stood looking at my battered old Underwood typewriter, and the only inspiration I felt was the one coming from my empty stomach. I abandoned the study for the kitchen before remembering that there was nothing there to eat. But, alas, May June had struck again. The refrigerator was stocked to overflowing: bologna, salami, two kinds of cheese, strawberry preserves, fresh vegetables, eggs, milk, a twelve-pack of Budweiser, a twelve-pack of diet Pepsi—how did she know?—a jar of instant coffee, and every condiment known to man. Several bags of munchies adorned the top of the fridge, and the cabinet over the sink was full of bread, cereal, sugar, flour, and the various box mixes that make up the necessities of the bachelor life.

I thanked God that May June Hall was old, fat, short, and married. Had she not been, I might have fallen madly in love with her on the spot.

Feeling highly invigorated at my good fortune, I made two bologna and American cheese sandwiches, popped a bag of Fritos and a can of Bud, turned my radio on to the only rock and roll station I could find, and went back to the study to work on my sermon.

Usually I spend at least a part of every day working on a sermon. But this was not the usual case. It was a maiden sermon at a new church, and I had only Friday afternoon and evening and Saturday to prepare it. So I reached into my files for one of what my ex-wife used to call my "ball breakers" and came up with "Hide and Seek."

It's a good sermon, maybe a great sermon, that listens better than it reads. Full of strong stories from my own experience, solid biblical references, and short, easy-to-take-home statements of faith. It still felt good as I read through it, and I decided that, with a few minor adjustments, it would do nicely for Sunday morning.

It was after 5:00 P.M. when I heard a knock at the front door of the parsonage. Shocked at the amount of time that had passed, I brushed the remains of my lunch into a grocery bag along with two beer cans, a diet Pepsi can, and an old bowl full of pipe ashes. I ducked into the bathroom and took a quick look in the medicine-cabinet mirror, found everything to be acceptable, if not great, and went to the door, fully expecting to find Ray Hall grinning through the screen.

I couldn't have been more wrong.

She was five-eight or so, with curly red hair that gave her face an innocent, childish look. Pale skin, green eyes, and a shy grin that gushed of sexuality. She had the body of an overdeveloped teenager and the face of a twenty-year-old. Almost invisible crow's-feet around her eyes said maybe thirty-five.

I wished, immediately, that I had been more critical during my trip to the bathroom mirror. A quick flick of the hairbrush, maybe. A splash of cologne. Anything.

And then she spoke, and much—not all, but much—of the beauty was gone.

"Praise the Lord, Reverend, and welcome to Baird!" It was a squeaky little-girl voice full of innocence that could not possibly be found in one of her age.

"Uh, hello" was all I could manage.

"You are the Reverend Thompson, aren't you?" she asked, her smile breaking into a big grin.

"Yes, I am. Can I help you?"

She brought her arm from behind her back and held up a picnic basket complete with red-checkered tablecloth covering the contents. "Well, you could open the door and invite me in. I'm Rachael Sites, your neighbor."

I managed to make my arms move and pushed the screen door out far enough for it to press up to her ample chest. "Mrs. Sites. Oh, well, thank you. I met Reverend Sites last night."

She giggled when the door touched her boobs, stepped back, took it, and glided easily into the house. "You did? Oh, shoot! I wanted to surprise you. I suppose he already told you all about me, then."

"Uh, well. I was with the constable, and we were there on business."

"Ray? You know Ray Hall. Ain't he cute? He's just a big old teddy bear, you know. I told May June, I said, you just keep an eye on that big teddy bear of a husband of yours or I'm liable to snuggle up to him and fall asleep and never let go." All this she said as she swept into the kitchen. It was a little disconcerting seeing this big, luscious woman sweeping through the house in jogging shorts and tank shirt and red hair and boobs flying everywhere and, at the same time, saying such inane things in that high-pitched childish voice.

". . . like roast beef," she was saying.

"I'm sorry?"

She laughed again. "You're just like Jerry! He never listens to a thing I say. I've prayed about it and asked the Lord to make him more attentive, but I guess he just has other plans for Jerry." She began taking things out of the basket and laying them on the counter between the sink and the refrigerator. "I said, I hope you like roast beef. I made it up into sandwiches. And I've got some potato salad and a thermos of fresh lemonade and a homemade cherry pie." She produced the pie and held it tilted so I could see it. It was burned around the edges and collapsed in the middle.

"It looks delicious," I lied.

"Well, now, there's a gentleman," she said, flirting openly. Then, just as quickly, she plopped the pie on the counter, closed her eyes, folded her hands beneath her breasts, and said, "Lord, I just want to thank you for sending this dear sweet man to us in our time of need. And I just ask that you bless him and annoint him for the task you've set before him." Her eyes popped open, and she smiled at me. "You don't know how I've prayed for the Lord to send another born-again Christian to this awful place. It's so hard being the only saved person in the whole township."

Of course. A born-again Christian. Ray had mentioned that fact and, the PTL greeting at the screen door should have tipped me off, but I didn't want to believe it.

"Well, I hope I can have an impact . . ." I began.

"It's him who has the impact," she said, looking at the ceiling. "All we can do is let him use us. Like me. I have given my body to the Lord. I jog and work out every day and eat the right things as a testimony to the godly life. The children at the home see me, and they say, if God can do that for her, he can do it for me. And they are led to holiness by my example, if it's what God wants for them."

I wanted to ask her why God wouldn't want children led to holiness and how it was, exactly, that her bra size had anything to do with all of that, but I thought it best not to challenge her. Born-again Christians are often easily offended by reason and logic. Besides, she was still talking.

". . . is a gift from God, just like some people have the gift of tongues and others have the gift of prophecy and others have the gift of music or business or athletic ability. This is my gift." She struck a classic Betty Grable pose.

"Before I knew the Lord, I wasted my gift. I was Miss Clermont County back in Ohio, and you know what I was going to do? I was going to go to Hollywood—*whore*lywood is what I call it now—and be an actress. Can you imagine that? What a terrible waste that would have been. Do you like mayonnaise? All I have is salad dressing, but I can't tell the difference in taste."

"Salad dressing is fine," I said. She had almost caught me off guard with the sudden shift in subject matter.

"Well, anyway, I met Jerry when I was at Ohio University studying theater arts. He was pastor of these three little churches there in the hills of Athens County."

"Was Jerry responsible for your conversion?" I swear I don't know why I asked this question. I did not want her in my kitchen. I did not want her in my house. I did not want to hear about her courtship. Call me uncharitable, but that's how it was. But I said it. It just slipped out.

Maybe it was because she was so different from Jerry Sites. He was probably ten years older than she was, and he was solid and practical, and if my judgment could be trusted, he was no born-again Christian. As much as I tended to like the guy, though, he seemed so . . . so guarded. His wife was anything but guarded. I had the feeling that before this conversation was over, she was going to tell me about her sex life. In fact, I had the distinct feeling that she was dying to tell me about her sex life.

But for now she was telling me about her conversion.

"No. Heavens," she said, giggling that little-girl giggle that seemed so out of place. She continued to slather salad dressing on the sandwiches. "No, Jerry hasn't met the Lord . . . yet. I think the Lord is saving Jerry for some very special purpose. But that's only natural, for a woman to feel that way about her husband. I mean, if I thought he was going to stay this way forever, I don't think I could live with him any longer. That's biblical, you know."

I didn't, but I let it pass.

"Don't you think that's sad? I mean, a minister who hasn't really come to know Jesus Christ as his personal Lord and Savior?" She looked as if she might begin weeping at any moment. "I've tried. God is my witness that I've tried to bring him to the Lord. I've dragged him to revivals and tent meetings and even into Perry to the First Baptist Church and the King's Road Assembly of God, but I swear he's the most stubborn man I've ever known. The Holy Ghost is going to have to work overtime to bring Gerald Sites around."

Suddenly she dropped the spatula, slapped the sandwiches back together, and folded her hands under her breasts again. She tilted her head back and closed her eyes. "Lord, I just want to thank you for this food and just ask once again that you will bring Jerry Sites, my husband, into your fold. I don't want him to burn in hell, Jesus. I want to be with him in paradise. Save him, Lord. Amen."

"Amen," I echoed, a little embarrassed.

Rachael placed the sandwiches on paper towels on the table, found two cracked saucers in the pantry, and dished up some potato salad for each of us. Lemonade went into two coffee mugs. We sat across from each other at the kitchen table, she on the edge of her chair. She ate in little tiny nibbles, dabbing the corners of mouth after every bite. I said my own prayer, thanking God that I didn't have to sit across the table from her at every meal. The little bites allowed her to continue a running monologue through the most of the meal.

"I don't want you to think I don't love him. Jerry is a wonderful man. He's kind and gentle and thoughtful and very affectionate. It's just that, well, I can't think of him as a Christian as long as he's so resistant to God's word. You know, 'ye must be born again,' or you cannot enter the kingdom of heaven."

"He seems like a fine man," I said. I know it was hardly a rebuke of her nonsense, but give me a break, I'd only known the woman for a few minutes.

"Oh, he is! That's right, you said you met him last night. Isn't he a doll? I hope you gave him your witness and prayed with him. It's so nice having another Christian to help me with him."

"Well, I was there with the constable. Sort of official business," I said.

"That's right! You said Teddy Bear Ray was there. Was it about that poor little LeAnn Bertke?"

"Yes, it was."

"Isn't that a shame." It wasn't really a question, but her inflection sought agreement, so I nodded. "Poor little thing. I'll tell you, Dan, that girl's like a little sister to me, and I'll never believe that she had anything to do with that fire."

"You know her?"

"Oh, heavens, yes. Didn't Jerry tell you? Why, she and I did everything together. I was a Big Sister back in Clermont County, Ohio, so when we realized that LeAnn needed some extra attention I just naturally volunteered."

"What kind of extra attention did she need?" I asked, wondering why Jerry hadn't told us about his wife's familiarity with the missing girl.

"Well, Dan, this is kind of embarrassing. I don't know how to say it, exactly." We were both finished with our sandwiches, and she got up and started for the cherry pie with a butter knife.

"Rachael, I've been a pastor for nearly fifteen years. There's nothing a person could tell me that would shock or embarrass me."

"Well, she was just a little bit of a thing when she came to us, but she was, oh, you know, flirty."

"Flirty?"

"More than flirty, actually. She was ... I know this sounds awful, but I can't think of a better word ... she was whorish. Does that make sense?"

"I think so."

"I mean, she would rub herself in public and brush her little boobies up against the boys to get what she wanted. She even tried it with Jerry a couple of times."

"So he came to you," I said, admiring the man's ability to handle a difficult situation.

"Yes, he did. And a good thing, too. I befriended her, and she seemed to get better after a while. Why, last year she was acting like a normal fifteen-year-old girl."

"But this year?"

"Something happened. I don't know what it was. Some of the kids said she fell in love with some boy and ran off with him. Some of them said her daddy had come back and taken her away. Some said she got pregnant and went off to Lexington to get an abortion. Anyway, she ran away."

"How long was she gone?" I asked.

"About a week," Rachael said, cutting into the pie. "How big a piece do you want?" Then, "Of pie, I mean." She giggled.

I said no, thanks, and patted my stomach.

"Oh, for heaven's sake, you're not fat."

"And I want to say that way. Maybe later," I said, knowing I'd throw the thing out as soon as she was gone.

"Well, okay." She cut herself a huge piece of pie and placed it on her potato salad saucer. It overlapped the edges by a good inch all the way around. "Anyway. No one knew where she had been, and she wouldn't talk about it. Then it happened two more times."

"Two more times? In a row?"

Her bites of pie were as big as her bites of sandwich were small. She dabbed at the corners of her mouth with the paper towel. "No, about three months apart. The first time was in, oh, October, I guess. Then again in February and the last time this last April."

"What did Reverend Sites say?"

"Oh, he was livid. I've never seen him so mad. When she came back the last time he told her if she ran off again she'd have to stay gone because she couldn't come back. She said she didn't give a good goddamn—sorry, Jesus—what he said because in June she'd turn sixteen and he wouldn't have any say over her anyhow. Jerry was hurt, I could tell."

"Did any other changes take place when she started running away?" I asked.

"Yeah," she answered, her mouth full of pie. "That's when she took to wearing those skimpy little outfits. Tube tops and see-through shirts and no underwear and what have you. Whorish, you know?"

"I think I'm beginning to get the picture," I said. And I was. For some reason, a sexually precocious twelve-year-old had put away adult things for two years, and then all of a sudden, about ten months ago, it had all come back again, with a vengeance. Why? What had happened?

I was going to ask Rachael her opinion on the subject, but someone was pounding, really pounding, on the front door.

I was hoping it would be Ray, back from the school with a report on what he'd found out from LeAnn Bertke's friends, but it wasn't him. It wasn't anyone. There was another picnic basket sitting on the stoop in front of the door. It was a little smaller than Rachael's but done up about the same—a gingham tablecloth bunched up over the goodies inside.

"Well, isn't that sweet," Rachael said from behind me. "These people! Aren't they just the sweetest, kindest people God ever made? They won't pay you much here, Dan, but you'll eat well."

I carried the basket to the kitchen and set it on the table. I'd take care of whatever was in it later. Right now I wanted to pump Rachael Sites, while she was in a talking mood, about whatever she knew about the missing LeAnn Bertke.

"I'll bet Alma Stevens did that. I think that's her gingham. I saw it at the church picnic last June. Aren't you gonna see what's in it?" Rachael asked.

"Later," I said. "Right now I'm full of that delicious roast beef you brought."

Rachael blushed and flipped her hand at me. "Oh, you."

"Would you like a cup of coffee, Rachael?" I asked, putting a small pan of water to boil on the stove. She said she would, and I rinsed out our lemonade mugs and put a spoon of instant into each one.

The water came quickly to boil, and I brought the steaming mugs to the table. Hot weather notwithstanding, I like a cup of coffee after a meal. Lots of sugar and milk if there's any around. There was, thanks to May June Hall.

"Rachael," I said, stirring my coffee, "where do you think LeAnn ran off to when she disappeared those times?"

She shrugged. "Lord, I wish I knew. I thought we were close, you know. Like sisters. Then she does a thing like that. It makes you wonder."

"She never mentioned it? Never talked about a place she might like to go if she ran away or wanted to be alone?" I asked.

"No, never. To tell the truth, after she ran away that first time we didn't spend too much time together. She always had something she had to do. At first I thought maybe I'd been too pushy."

"Too pushy? About what?"

"About Jesus!" she said, as if I were a naughty schoolboy with whom a teacher was losing her patience. "I was trying to bring her to the Lord. But she was as resistant as Jerry. I thought maybe I had pushed her away by trying too hard, you know?"

"But something changed your mind?"

"Yeah. Now I think she was off with that Taylor boy, what's his name?"

"Adam?"

"Yeah, that's him."

"What makes you say that?"

"Well, look at him! He's rich! What sixteen-year-old girl in her prime and pretty as LeAnn is wouldn't want to latch on to him. I told her he wasn't any good. I told her, 'That Adam Taylor just wants to get into your panties and then dump you like he does all his girls.' But it's hard to talk sense to a sixteen-year-old girl who's in love."

"Adam's a ladies' man?" I asked matter-of-factly.

"Oh, Lord, that one. Yes, he's a killer. Pretty as a movie star and vain as a peacock. Driving that big dump truck around like a maniac and spending his daddy's money like there's no tomorrow. Little thing like LeAnn, all she can see is he's got a bulge in his hip pocket and a bulge behind his zipper and she thinks she's in love. Well, I coulda told her there's more to love that that, a whole heck of a lot more." She was picking up crumbs of pie with the tip of her index finger and licking them slowly off. It looked erotic as hell.

"What is it with kids, Dan? Can you tell me? You take a little thing like LeAnn and you give her two years of your life. Kindness, gentleness, affection, self-confidence, pride in herself, companionship. Then one day her hormones kick in and she sees some boy she thinks is the whole world, and just because he's got a penis she decides that everything you did for her is just so much trash and she throws it right back in your face. What is it about kids that makes them do that?" She licked her finger one last time and pushed the plate away, disgusted.

"Rachael, if you could stop that from happening, you would make mothers of teenage girls the happiest people in the world. And the human race would probably die out in about twenty years because none of the daughters would ever move out and get married." I drank the last of my coffee and burped. I'd made it too strong. Probably have heartburn in the night. "Excuse me," I added, behind the burp.

She waved off my apology. "Well, if you ask me, that Adam Taylor's the one Ray Hall oughta be looking for. He's no good. He's just out to use LeAnn and throw her away. And there's something wrong with him and that big friend of his. They ... I don't know ... like to hurt things."

I didn't ask what she meant, just raised my eyebrows and made a question mark out of my face.

"Like that time he was driving through town here," she said by way of explanation. I had the feeling this was something of a confession for her, because she was having trouble keeping eye contact with me. "There was this little dog—just a pup, really—and it was laying in the shade by the porch down at the diner ..."

She stopped talking, and her eyes slowly got as big as the saucer she'd eaten her pie from. The memory, I reasoned, must be a painful one for her. Either that or she had just thought of something that might shed some light on what we were talking about. But then I realized that she was not going to finish the sentence.

It was just hanging there. She had forgotten what she was talking about. And her eyes weren't focused like those of a person trying to visualize something from the past. They were focused completely and totally just to my left, on the basket I had brought in from the front stoop. It was sitting less than an arm's reach from where we both sat, and I had nearly forgotten that it was there.

I followed her gaze and noticed that the gingham tablecloth was moving, rippling really, as if a small earthquake was going on inside the basket.

"What the hell," I said and reached out to pull off the gingham cover but yanked my hand back just as quickly. A diamond-shaped head about the size of a small teacup eased itself smoothly from under one of the folds. A forked tongue popped in and out of the mouth. The head became a neck, and the neck became a body with brown and tan hourglass patterns on its back as the snake eased itself effortlessly from the basket and onto the kitchen table.

Rachael erupted from her seat screaming, and I shot out of my chair, sending it crashing to the floor, and backed halfway across the kitchen. The noise must have confused the snake, because it raised its head and seemed to look around in all directions, finally deciding to investigate the sound vibrations coming from near the sink.

The sound was Rachael's scream. I don't think she had taken a breath. The scream was one long, continuous screech, and now, as the snake made its way toward her, she began to shake and dance in place. She was backed up against the sink, the table in front of her, her overturned chair blocking her on the right. She could have eased her way to the left, but she wasn't thinking. She was frozen in panic. A wet stain blossomed on the front of her running shorts and I could hear liquid falling on the floor.

I looked around the kitchen, desperate for something, anything, with which to divert the snake's attention, but there was nothing within reach. The knives, pots, and pans were all on the counter and stove behind Rachael. I could feel myself beginning to freeze in panic and uncertainty and tried to shake it off. I had to do something or I would soon not be able to do anything. Any action would be better than just standing there watching the snake inch its way toward Rachael.

I backed up and picked up the aluminum and vinyl chair I had been sitting in and raised it above my head. The snake was now on the edge of the table, maybe a foot from Rachael. The chair was awkward and not a very good club. If I didn't hit the snake just right I might simply knock it off the table onto the floor or, worse, onto Rachael. But the chair was all I had, so I prepared to use it. Maybe a sideways glancing blow would knock the viper back across the table. If I didn't kill it, at least I'd knock it away from Rachael so I could grab her and get her out of the kitchen.

I tensed my arms and tried to find an angle that would knock the snake toward the living room. Not good, but better than nothing. I visualized where the chair would hit, rose up on tiptoes to put everything I had into the swing, and an explosion erupted in the kitchen, deafening me. The snake disappeared in a blast of blood and whatever else snakes are made up of. A massive scar appeared on the table where it had been. Rachael fainted and fell into a pool of her own urine on the floor.

I felt my arms begin to tremble and weaken, and then the chair was removed from my grasp and placed on the floor behind me.

"I see you got one, too," Ray Hall said from behind me. He had come in from the office that led to the church. "You better sit down, Reverend. You look a little peaked." He leaned a .410 single-shot shotgun against the counter and went over to check on Rachael. "Lord god A'mighty, Rachael, you pissed yourself," he said, but Rachael couldn't hear him.

I could barely hear him myself. My ears were ringing from the report of the shotgun in the small kitchen, and there were little silver specks flickering in front of my eyes, and the kitchen seemed suddenly very hot, and I was feeling dizzy. . . .

I fainted and fell out of the chair.

I knew I was fainting, knew I was falling, knew I was feeling awfully stupid, and there wasn't a damn thing I could do about it. The last thing I heard before my head smacked against the floor was Ray's voice.

"Aw, shit, Dan. Not you, too. . . ."

Women faint and it's no big deal. They've been doing it in movies for years. You may not expect it, but you accept it with a shrug and a knowing look.

Men faint and they're assholes or woosies.

The fact that Ray and Jerry Sites didn't treat me like an asshole or a woosie did not change the fact that I felt like one. I woke up on the threadbare couch in the living room with a splitting headache and an upset stomach. My shirt was soaked with perspiration, and my mouth was as dry as cotton.

And Jerry Sites was upside down.

"You okay?" he asked. He was standing above me at the end of the couch, looking down.

I said, "Yeah," but it hurt my head to say it, so I let it go at that.

"Your head hit the floor when you fell. You got a goose egg as big as . . . a goose egg," he said, smiling sheepishly.

"Rachael?"

"She's okay. Kind of embarrassed, but she'll be fine. May June gave her some tea and took her up to the house." He walked around the end of the couch and sat on the scarred coffee table. "I heard the screams and the shot and ran down here. Helped Ray get you on the couch. Here." He handed me a dish towel filled with ice cubes, and I put it against my goose egg.

"Where's Ray?" I said, my head clearing a little with the cold.

"He's out in the kitchen, lookin' over that basket."

I tried to sit up but fell back when the room started to go around in circles. "I touched it," I said. "Brought it in from the porch. My fingerprints."

"Don't worry about fingerprints." Ray walked from the kitchen and came around to where I could see him towering above me. "We'd have to send them to Lexington, and it'd take three weeks to get 'em back. Stuff like that isn't much use out here."

Jerry Sites stood and straightened his slacks. "I guess I better get on up to the house and check on Rachael. Funny, I was wondering where she was. I didn't know she was on her way down here. She usually leaves me a note or something." He shrugged and walked to the front door. "Y'all take care, now."

The cold from the ice cubes was helping my head a great deal, but the meltwater was dripping all over me and the couch, so I tried to sit up again and, after one false start, made it. The dizziness was gone, but the pain was still there like tiny explosions going off right where I parted my hair.

Ray came in, took the towel, and carried it into the kitchen, then came back with a bottle of aspirin and a bottle of brandy.

"Where'd you get that?" I asked, figuring May June had brought it with the tea she gave to Rachael.

"Aspirin's in the cupboard over the sink. Brandy's in the cabinet under the sink," he said. He poured three fingers of the liquor into a coffee mug and shook out five aspirin into the palm of his hand and gave it all to me.

"Under the sink?" I asked, gulping the concoction. The brandy threatened to come back up then settled down and started to warm me all over.

"Yeah. May June always puts the preacher's liquor under the sink with the cleaning stuff. Looks more medicinal that way."

"Thank her for me," I said.

"Well, it's cheap, but it knocks the hell out of a chill." He smiled.

The aspirin was going to take a while to kick in, but the brandy was doing fine. It stopped the shakes and cleared my vision. I really, really wanted another, but Ray had capped the bottle and was on his way toward the kitchen. Just as well. Tomorrow I would move the brandy to somewhere harder to reach. Just in case. For now I just leaned back, closed my eyes, and put my feet up on the coffee table.

"You said something just before I passed out," I called into the kitchen.

He came back carrying two mugs of coffee. "I said, 'Oh, shit, Dan. Not you, too.'" I took one mug of coffee, and he took the other to the reading chair in front of the window.

"No, before that. Right after you shot the snake."

"Oh, that. I said that you got one, too."

"One what? Snake?"

He nodded. "Second one tonight."

"Who else got one?" I asked, alarm sneaking into my voice.

"Don't know," he said, shrugging. "It was in LeAnn Bertke's locker up to the school. Big diamondback. Don't know who it was intended for. Maybe her. Maybe anyone who opened the locker."

"Why?"

He shrugged again. He was slinking lower and lower into his chair. "Joke, maybe. Maybe just to scare people."

I shuddered. "Well, it worked. It scared the shit out of me."

"Scared somethin' else outta Rachael," he said, a small smile playing across his face.

"It wasn't funny, Ray. She was terrified."

"No, I reckon it weren't. Still . . ."

"Why don't you like the Siteses?"

I waited while he went through his cigarette ritual. When he finally had one going, he spoke. "I guess it's not that I don't like 'em. I just don't trust 'em."

I let it lie there. Good pastoral technique: don't pump; just encourage people to talk by not interrupting.

Ray blew out a stream of smoke. "He's a pompous ass, and she's a dim bulb," he said. "You ever seen a born-again Christian dress and act like her?"

"Well . . ."

"Dresses like a tart and talks like a two-dollar whore and then wants everyone to believe she's a virgin, pure as driven snow. Shit."

"Does she fool around?" I couldn't help thinking of my own reaction to the woman. One minute I was sure she was coming on to me, licking her finger, giggling over double entendres. The next minute I was certain that she didn't know she was having any effect on me at all. She was a sexual paradox.

"Damned if I know. But I wouldn't put a five-dollar bet on her saying no if it was offered. I'd steer clear, I were you."

"You mean, given my record and all . . ."

"You ain't the first man in the world let his dick do his thinkin' for him. I'd just hate to see it happen again, and with her it's even money."

"I don't know," I said. "I've seen women like her before, Ray. They have no intention of coming across on their implied offers. She just likes to see the look on a man's face when he finds her desirable. Something in her ego needs that."

"Maybe. And maybe somethin' in her panties needs somethin' else."

"What's all this got to do with LeAnn Bertke or that snake in my kitchen?" I asked, trying to change the subject.

"Don't know that, either," he said, sitting up. "Just talkin's all. It's a ponder, that's for sure."

"Do you think LeAnn did it?" I asked. "You think she's mad about something, or on a rampage?"

Ray sat up in the chair and massaged his temples. "Could be, but she's got no call to kill you. She doesn't even know you. And the snake up to the school wasn't aimed at anyone in particular. Just the first person to open the locker."

"So you don't think it's LeAnn?"

"Didn't say that. I think it probably is. I just wish I knew why."

"She's crazy," I said. It seemed so obvious.

"Or she's in love. It could just as easy be Adam Taylor warning us off. Or maybe it was whoever set the fire up at the Martin place. Or maybe someone we haven't even thought of yet."

I lay back down on the couch and closed my eyes. The pain in my head hadn't subsided in the slightest, and the nausea was coming back. I had every intention of telling Ray what I had learned from Rachael Sites, but right then I just didn't have the energy or the fortitude. "I came up here to be a simple country preacher, Ray. Why can't anything be simple or easy anymore?"

"I'll guess with ya," he said, standing. He collected the coffee mugs and walked toward the kitchen. "You need anything else?"

"A new head," I managed to murmur. I let my arm fall across my eyes and heard him clip off the overhead light.

"I'll let myself out," he said. A few minutes later I heard the screen door slam, then the outer door. Ray rattled the knob to make sure it was locked. The quiet of the house and the mountains outside swallowed me, and for the second night in my new parsonage I slept on the couch in the living room.

I might as well be married, I thought as I drifted off.

I dreamed of my ex-wife.

She was standing in the kitchen of my parsonage in exactly the same spot where Rachael Sites had been standing, and there was a snake on the kitchen table moving slowly toward her. Only she didn't scream. She bitched.

She complained about snakes and how she hated them and how this was just her luck to find a big snake in her kitchen. And it was a big snake, maybe ten times bigger than the copperhead that had been intended for me—python size—and it kept crawling toward her, but she wouldn't move. She just stood there bitching.

I had Ray's shotgun, and I kept aiming it at the snake and pulling the trigger, but the damn thing wouldn't fire, and she just kept bitching, and finally I aimed the gun at her and was this close to pulling the trigger . . . and I woke up.

Freud would, no doubt, have had a field day. I did not. Sometimes a snake is just a snake and a gun is just a gun.

The second time I woke up it was to the sounds of dogs barking. Baying, really. But it was an awful racket and it didn't help the pain in my head, which now came as much from sleeping on the couch as from the shrinking lump on my temple.

I was still in my clothes from the day before, so I pulled on an old pair of running shoes, went to investigate, and found the Carmack twins standing in front of the diner chewing tobacco and looking as homely as ever. Three dogs were tied in the back of the pickup truck the twins were leaning against—a beagle, a bloodhound, and something that looked like a cross between a Dalmation and a beagle. All three of the dogs acted as if they had never been outside before and were really excited about this opportunity.

"Morning, guys," I said as I walked by. It was already getting hot in the sun, and my head and stomach could stand no more conversation than that.

"Morning, Reverend," the twins said simultaneously, and nodded their heads solemnly. They assumed I was talking to them and not to the dogs.

May June was behind the counter in the diner and poured me a cup of coffee as soon as she saw me come through the door. "How's the head?" she asked as I sat down. She leaned across the counter and began examining my scalp as though my report could not possibly be accurate enough to suit her.

"It hurts like a mother," I said.

Her examination completed, she nodded with satisfaction. "Mmh" was all she said. "You look like hell. Want some eggs?"

"What time is it?"

"Seven-thirty. You want some eggs?"

"Just some dry toast, thanks. My stomach's a little upset."

"No wonder," she said, shaking her head. "He said he gave you some brandy. Fool. That's for winter. A warm quilt woulda done better. Brandy just makes you feel warm, but it don't warm ya. An' it sets your stomach on edge, especially on top of one of Rachael Sites's world-famous roast beef sandwiches."

"I think it's just the headache that's doing it," I said irrationally trying to defend Ray and Rachael. "What's going on?"

"I ain't sure. Ray's on the phone to his cousin the sheriff again. He'll be mad when he comes out. He always is after he talks to that little putz." She slid two pieces of Wonder bread out of a sack on the counter, smeared butter on them, and plopped them on the hot griddle. Appalachian version of dry toast, I supposed.

"Putz, May June?"

"Yeah, putz. I heard that on 'Seinfeld' and it's a perfect word for Sheriff William B. Fine, thankya."

"And they say television isn't educational," I said, trying to laugh.

Ray emerged from the constable's office just as I was finishing the country toast. May June had dropped a tablespoon of honey on each piece, and it was working miracles on my upset stomach. I was beginning to think that perhaps I had mistaken hunger for nausea, so good was I feeling. But it would take more than toast and honey to make Ray feel good. He was smoldering.

"Do you always look like that after you talk to your cousin?" I asked.

"No," he growled, picking up a mug that had been sitting on the counter and tasting the contents. He made a face and pushed the mug away. "Usually I'm in a bad mood."

"What's going on?"

"Well, Sheriff William B. Shit-for-Brains Fine has decided that LeAnn Bertke is lost in the woods on Pine Tree Mountain and we should track her with Gilbert Carmack's dogs. Jesus!"

May June cleared her throat and handed a mug of fresh coffee across the counter to Ray. "Dad, couldn't you please control your language a little?"

"Yeah, sure, I wouldn't want to offend anyone," Ray said absently. He sipped his coffee.

"Well, he is a minister, after all. And I don't care if he is a regular guy like you say, it just doesn't seem right."

The fact that Ray had, at some time, told May June that he considered me a regular guy did even more good for my stomach than May June's toast.

"All right, Mother. I'll try to watch it."

"You don't think she's in the bush on Pine Tree

Mountain?" I asked, trying to move the conversation along and away from Ray's language, which had offended me not at all.

"Well, I guess it's a possibility. But a damn slim one. See, Dan, everyone thinks of Appalachia, and they think of the Foxfire books. They think of mountain people living in log cabins and livin' off the land, using folk remedies and cherished family secrets, eatin' herbs and shit. Sorry, Mother."

May June shook her head and sipped her own coffee.

"The thing is," Ray continued, "most Appalachians got no more knowledge of the mountains than anyone else. Oh, they like 'em an' all, and they may hunt them if they haven't hunted them out, but what they know about living off the land you could write on your thumbnail.

"Mostly, we work in towns or coal mines, we watch TV, we drive cars, we try to keep body and soul together. We drive to Perry and do our shopping at supermarkets just like everyone else. Hell, the first time someone even told me about the Foxfire books I thought they were talking about that spy novel about that super-fast plane. That Clint Eastwood movie, remember?"

"Firefox," I said, drawing on my storehouse of trivia.

"Right. Hell, I can pick out a sassafras tree and an oak and a maple, but that's about it. And a sixteen-year-old girl ain't even gonna be able to do that. If she's out there in the bush, she's been there for two nights, and there ain't no way she's still alive."

"So you think this is a waste of time," I said, more of a statement than a question.

"I damn well know it is! Stupid shit-for-brains little idjit. But he's the boss so I gotta do it."

"Ray, I had a long talk with Rachael Sites last night over roast beef sandwiches," I said. "She told me some things."

"I'll bet she did," he said, taking some more coffee.

"No, I mean about LeAnn Bertke. It wasn't in a counseling context, so I don't think I would be violating a confidence if I shared it with you. Besides, it's sort of weird."

Ray didn't really ask me to tell him; he just raised his eyebrows at me and settled himself on the stool at the counter, and I took that as an invitation to tell all, which I did. I told him about Rachael's claim that she was LeAnn's big sister and how Jerry Sites had asked her to befriend LeAnn after the younger girl had shown signs of early sexual promiscuity. I told him about Rachael's claim that LeAnn had turned around and straightened out until this past year and then started acting like a sex fiend again. And I told him about the three disappearances. For a story that seemed so important, it only took a couple of minutes to tell. As Ray went through his cigarette ritual I wondered if maybe I hadn't given too much importance to the whole thing.

Finally Ray spoke: "Maybe ol' Jerry wasn't the only one gettin' into little LeAnn's pants."

"Well, the trips away would seem to indicate that something might have been going on between her and the Taylor boy," I said, pointing out what I thought was only obvious.

"Yeah," Ray said, nodding. "But I wasn't talking about him."

"Who else?"

"Mrs. Sites. Mrs. Hot Pants Thank You Jesus."

"Oh, for God's sake, Ray. Just because you don't like the Siteses doesn't mean ..." But I couldn't go on. It was possible. Maybe Rachael's sex-bomb thing was just an act. Maybe Jerry had set the fox in charge of the henhouse.

"Whadaya think?" Ray asked, trying to read my face.

"Well, I suppose it's possible."

"Anything's possible, Reverend," he said with a sigh. "Even as little police work as I do's taught me that." He turned to May June. "Mother, you remember Fay Parkerson and her daughter?"

May June nodded, then shook her head. "Now, you don't know about them for sure, Ray. Don't go spreading gossip about the dead."

"Gossip my ass." He turned back to me. "Woman and her grown-up daughter lived over in Skinnerd Valley. She was a divorcée, and the daughter was an old maid. Mom in her late fifties, daughter in her late thirties. Both women healthy and strong as horses, kinda homely. Dad took off one summer for no good reason, and no one ever saw him again.

"Well, we had a cold snap early one September before anyone had their firewood cut, and Fay, she's so stupid she just dumps a bunch of charcoal briquettes into the fireplace and lights 'em up before bedtime. They didn't show up in church the next day, so their minister goes out on Monday to call on 'em and there they are in the same bed deader'n doornails, both of 'em."

"Ray, they mighta just been tryin' to stay warm," May June said. "It was a bad cold snap."

Ray winked at me. "They was both stark necked," he said. "The preacher near had a conniption."

I just shook my head. You never can tell about some people. May June snorted and collected the coffee mugs.

"Oh, that ain't all," Ray said, smiling. "We found the husband's body under the house. Well, not the body, really. Just the bones. Lord, how'd they stand the stink?"

I wrinkled my face in disgust. "You mean they . . ."

"Killed him, stuck him under the house, and commenced bein' lovers. Mother and daughter." He crossed his arms. "Now you tell me somethin' ain't possible."

"Anything's possible, Ray," I admitted.

"Sure is. Whoever it was LeAnn was runnin' off with, this might lead us to him . . . or her." He pulled something out of his pocket and slapped it on the counter. It was a flap of matches from the Sawyer Motel in Perry. "Found that under a bunch of crap in the bottom of LeAnn's locker. I'll check it out tomorrow, after the sheriff's hunt."

I picked up the matchbook and put it in my shirt pocket. "I have to drive in to Perry this afternoon to see about the Martins' funeral. Why don't I check out the motel for you?"

Ray smiled again and handed me the picture of LeAnn. "I was hopin' you'd say that," he said

It's only thirty miles from Baird to Perry, the county seat, but it takes over an hour to drive it. The main road through Baird, State Route 42, is a two-lane asphalt highway that twists and turns and follows the natural valley through the mountains along the Pitts River.

I didn't arrive in Perry until a little before noon. I had taken a shower and put on my summer preacher's suit, a lightweight cotton khaki job, a white shirt, and a black tie. I hadn't been kidding Ray about having business in the county seat.

First, I had to find the coroner's office and ask about the Martins and their funeral wishes. Second, I had to go over to the county clerk's office, show him my credentials, register as a duly ordained minister in the state of Kentucky, and apply for a license to solemnize marriages.

After these things were taken care of, I would drive over to the Sawyer Motel and inquire if anyone there remembered seeing LeAnn Bertke back in April. It was a long shot, but it might give Ray something to go on, and I wanted to help if I could, not only because of LeAnn but for the Martins and for myself. Try as I might, I could not erase from my mind the picture of that copperhead coiled on my kitchen table.

The sheriff's department was on the first floor of the courthouse, which stood in the very center of town, complete with a big front yard, park benches, a cannon, a war memorial, and some old men fanning themselves and swapping lies on the steps. Saturday must have been a slow crime day in Durel County as there was only one deputy on duty as far as I could tell, and he was drinking a Dr Pepper and reading a Sergeant Rock comic book when I walked in. He directed me to the basement of the county hospital, where the morgue was located, and when I went there, a cleancut military-looking morgue attendant directed me to the Whiteker Funeral Home on South Birch Street, where the Martins' bodies were scheduled to be sent on Monday morning.

LeRoy Whiteker was about thirty years old, taller than me, thinner than me, and, with his bright blue eyes and easy smile, as handsome as any man I'd ever met. His three kids were playing Monopoly on the floor of a viewing room in the front of the big white air-conditioned house that served as both his home and his business establishment.

"The Martins didn't leave any instructions that I know of," he said as he led me into his office. He wore a golf shirt and cotton slacks and had an easy, friendly manner that put me instantly at ease. "They were members of your church, and I just assumed they

125

would want to be laid out at the church and buried at the Pine Tree Mountain Cemetery."

"Is that how it's usually done?" I asked. There was a sign in his office that said No Smoking, but he had placed a circle and a slash through the "No." We both pulled out our pipes simultaneously.

"Most of the mountain folks want to be laid out in their church and buried near home. I know it's not easy for you, being new and having to deal with this, first thing. Is there anything I can do to help?"

"You're doing it right now. Thanks for the concern. Did the Martins have any survivors?"

"None that I know of. No kids of their own. That's why they took in kids from the children's home all the time."

"Who's paying for the funeral?"

"It will be paid for by the county, from the estate. I get a set fee."

I set my pipe on the desk to let the bowl cool. "From what I saw, there wasn't much left of the estate."

"They had a small savings account and a CD, according to Percy Mills, their lawyer."

"Would I seem nosy if I asked . . ."

"About thirty thousand dollars, I think. I was nosy, too. Probably their life savings. The funeral will cost about two grand. It'll be nice but not extravagant. I don't know who gets the rest. That nosy I'm not. Besides, I don't need to get rich off county funerals."

A little blond girl with a ponytail and Nike high-tops stormed into the office and ran up to his chair. "Dad," she whined, "Brian says you don't get five hundred dollars if you land on Go! Is that right? I just landed on Go, and I thought you got five hundred dollars if you landed on it."

LeRoy tried to hide a smile. "You collect five hundred dollars for landing on Go only if you are under eight years old and it's Saturday," he said to the little girl.

She looked pensive. "Really?"

"Reverend Thompson, is that not the official rule?" He had managed to swallow the smile and was now dead serious.

"Well," I said, matching his serious demeanor, "that's if you're playing by the East Coast rules." I turned to the little girl. "You are playing by the East Coast rules, aren't you?"

She looked at her dad, who nodded solemnly. "I would never allow my children to play by the West Coast rules," he said. "Scandalous what those Californians have done to the game."

The little blonde seemed to be lost. "Does that mean I get the five hundred dollars?" she asked.

"It does," LeRoy said and smiled at her.

"All right!" She turned and dashed from the room, shouting. "Brian!"

"That's Trisha, my youngest," Whiteker said. "She's seven, Brian's ten, and Molly's twelve." He seemed to brighten with each name.

"They're great kids," I said, suddenly missing my own. "Mine live with their mother."

"Divorced?"

"Two years. She moved to California last year and married a lawyer. I see my kids at Christmas and on my vacation every summer."

"It must be tough," he said, and I could tell that

he meant it. Separation would probably have killed a father like him. It had nearly killed me at first.

"It ain't easy." Then silence as we pondered the whole miserable business of divorce. He was kind enough to break the quiet.

"Of course, the Martins won't be laid out, what with the burns and all. But I suppose we'll still have the funeral at the church if that's okay with you."

"That's what the church is for," I said. "It's fine with me."

"Tuesday morning okay?"

"Tuesday's fine. About ten?"

"I'll be there. I'll take care of everything else—getting the graves dug and all." We both stood, pocketed our pipes, and shook hands. "Stop in any time you're in town, Dan. We'll have a burger or something."

I said that I would, and I meant it. I liked him.

The August heat hit me as though I had stepped into a furnace when I went back outside, so I decided not to brave the interior of the VW. The center of town was only three blocks away, and the walk would do me good. I took off my coat and slung it over my shoulder, picked up the sack lunch that May June had prepared for me, now cooked to mush in the VW, and headed back to the cool front yard of the courthouse.

As I walked, I thought about thirty thousand dollars—two or three years' pay in Durel County, providing you were lucky enough to have a job and belong to a union. I wondered if someone was going to land on Go as a result of the death of the Martins.

East Coast or West Coast rules? I wondered. The

lawyer's name was Percy Mills, I remembered. He would know.

The front yard of the courthouse was about half the size of a football field and also served as a city park for the small town. Benches, concrete picnic tables, a flagpole, and even a couple of pigeons decorated a scene that would have set Norman Rockwell to salivating.

I bought a diet Pepsi and a bag of chips from a diner across the street and sat on one of the benches in the shade to eat lunch. Everything in the bag was ruined except the Swiss cheese on rye sandwich, and it was melted to perfection. I didn't realize how hungry I was until I took the first bite and then another and another until my mouth was so full I could hardly chew.

"A little hot for a picnic, ain't it?" a feminine voice said from beside me. For a moment I was afraid it would be one of those embarrassing moments when a minister meets one of his parishioners away from the church and can't remember the name that goes with the slightly familiar face.

It was a stupid thought, though. I knew exactly four of my parishioners, and two of them were dead. The other two were the Halls, and this was not May June's voice. It was familiar, however.

"You not speakin' to me because of the way I treated you the other day?"

It was Naomi Taylor, and I was not speaking to her because my mouth was full of Swiss cheese sandwich. Besides, she was wearing a sundress that would have left me speechless in any event. It was orange and red and yellow and looked like it had been poured over her.

"Oh, hi," I said, swallowing my sandwich without further chewing and jumping to my feet. "Naomi, right?" As though I was having trouble remembering her name. Fat chance.

"Yeah. You decide to spend the day in the big city?" Her smile was genuine now. Nothing teasing or mischievous, so I relaxed.

"Oh, I had some errands to run. Just taking a break in the shade here. Join me?" I scooted over on the bench, leaving her a full two-thirds of it. She sat in the middle, her thigh almost touching mine. My heart nearly stopped.

"What kinda errands?"

"I had to check on the Martin funeral and get my license to marry. And I promised to look into a couple of things for Ray Hall."

"You gettin' married?"

For a second I didn't understand. Then it took. "Oh, no, not that kind of license. It's a license that ministers have to have to solemnize marriages. It's different in every state. I have to show my ordination papers to the county clerk," I said, pumping my thumb toward the courthouse.

She smiled again. "Not today. It's Saturday. Won't be anyone workin' today."

I'd forgotten about that. Shit. Another trip.

"But I know Elias. The deputy on duty? I'll see if he can take care of it for you," she said.

I shook my head. "No, it has to be the clerk. But if he can get me the form to fill out, I can make a copy of my ordination certificate and leave it for the clerk. Do you think he could?"

She shrugged. "Sure. He's got a crush on me. He will if I ask him."

She was carrying some bags with stores' names on them, and I nodded toward them. "Shopping?"

"Yeah. It's kind of a Saturday ritual here. Everyone who's got a dime to spend comes to Perry on Saturday and spends it. Sometimes you come even if you don't have a dime to spend, and you just walk around and hang out in the park. Pick up the latest gossip."

"Get any bargains?" I asked, not because I really cared, but because I wanted the conversation to continue. This was a lady upon whom even sweat was becoming.

"Nah. You want real bargains you got to drive to Lexington or sometimes Corbin. Down here they charge you a whole bag o' beans for everything. They have to 'cause they don't do enough volume. I did all right, though."

"How is your father?" I asked, feeling a little guilty for the state we had left him in.

"Oh, he's Daddy. You know. I don't know why he gets himself so worked up. Everyone knows Adam was seein' that little gal from the home, and Daddy acts like it's some big secret that he's got to protect his family's honor and all."

"I felt bad about the other day. The way we left him."

"Oh, you shouldn't. It was the heat as much as it was you two. I know Ray Hall wouldn't hurt anyone or anything on purpose in this world." She looked sideways at me and grinned. Dimples popped into her chin and cheek. "And I think you're probably okay, too," she said.

I smiled back and wondered if any rye bread was caught in my teeth. "Thanks. You're okay yourself."

She stood and collected her bags. "Well, let's go see if Elias can get you the papers you need."

We did and he could. Just barely.

It's embarrassing to watch a full-grown man fawn over a woman, even one as fetching as Naomi Taylor, and I was fully embarrassed for the poor oaf. Naomi smiled and asked sweetly for the papers I needed, and good old Elias stumbled into the clerk's office, unlocked a filing cabinet, found the papers, and turned on the photocopying machine for us. Then he promised to see to it personally that my license application got to the right person. When we walked out, he came outside and leaned against one of the big pillars in front of the courthouse and watched us walk away. That is, he watched her walk away. I doubted he would even remember my name. It was kind of sad.

"I think Elias is in love," I said.

She giggled. "Yeah. I was in love with him once, too. When we were both in high school. He was quarterback on the football team, and I was a cheerleader. The perfect couple."

"What happened?"

"I went off to college, and he got married. He's got three kids and a wife who weighs two hundred pounds. And he's in love with what we were, not who I am." She shrugged her shoulders again, a move that threatened to bring her breasts right up out of the halter top of her sundress. "It's kind of sad. About him, I mean. Not about us. If I had married him, I'd be the one who weighed two hundred pounds and cooked him his grits every morning."

I didn't have anything else to say, so I just helped

her stash her packages in the trunk of the big LTD that had been parked in her driveway the day before.

She was a strange and wonderful package. Beautiful and wholesome—close enough to a brunette Daisy Mae to turn most of the male heads on the courthouse lawn. But she was smart and headstrong, too. Smart enough not to get married to a hometown boy with "Nowhere" written on his career ticket.

"So what's next?" she said, slamming the trunk lid. "Elias isn't watching anymore, so we can do whatever we want. How 'bout an ice cream?"

"Well, I have those things I have to do for Ray. . . ."

"What are they?"

"I have to check something out at the Sawyer Motel and talk to a lawyer named Percy Mills, about the Martin estate."

"Okay," she said, looking over the courthouse lawn. "Percy Mills is out of town today, so you can't talk to him. The motel thing we can take care of after the ice cream."

"Do you know everybody in town?" I asked.

"Almost everybody. See that building over there? The fabric store?" She pointed across the square to a little storefront with several bolts of different colored gingham in the windows, and I nodded that, yes, I saw it. "Well, Percy Mills's office is in that building, above the fabric store. He owns the building, and his wife runs the store."

"Great. He's close. But how do you know he's out of town?" I asked, still looking at the storefront.

"If Percy was in town he'd either be in his office right in front of that window, which he isn't, or he'd be right over there." She pointed at a park bench on the lawn just across from the store. "He gets more

133

clients sittin' on that bench than he does in his office. He calls it his own personal courtroom. He's not at either place, so he must be out of town. Probably in Lexington, helping his wife pick up fabric and supplies for her store. She's not working today, either. That I know because I bought some fabric this morning."

"You still didn't say how you knew him," I said, giving her my own sideways look.

"He's Daddy's lawyer," she said, smiling. "He's about a hundred years old, and I've known him all my life. So let's go check out the motel. Come on, I'll drive you."

She had me stand outside of the LTD until the air conditioner brought the temperature down to the midnineties, and then she drove me through town, stopping for a Dairy Queen and pointing out where the best bargains were, where the honest mechanics worked, and where to buy clothing if you didn't have time to drive to Lexington.

Finally we pulled to a stop in front of a little motel made of concrete blocks painted aquamarine with sea horses on every door. There were about thirty rooms in all and a big front yard with a swimming pool that had long ago stopped being used. The grass in the yard had been cut but not raked, and weeds grew up waist high in the fence around what had been the pool. At close inspection, I could see that the aquamarine paint was peeling from the walls.

All in all, I would put the place just one millimeter this side of seedy.

The thing that saved it, the thing that provided that one millimeter, was the lady who stood behind the registration counter in the office that was also the foyer of an efficiency apartment.

She smelled strongly of roses, and she wore a house-dress, and her bifocals dangled from a chain around her neck. When I walked in with Naomi, she gave us a genuine smile and winked at me. I figured that her dirty mind and that wink were worth at least a millimeter.

"Can I help you, sir?"

"I hope so, ma'am. My name's Daniel Thompson. I'm the pastor of Baird Methodist Church, and we're looking for a little girl who's disappeared."

"Oh, dear. That's so tragic. I see that all the time. On milk cartons and on that television show and all." Her gaze drifted back to Naomi, and I saw something like a question in her eyes, so I answered it.

"This is Miss Taylor. She's a member of my parish." She and Naomi exchanged hellos while I fished the picture of LeAnn Bertke out of my suit jacket. I laid it on the counter. "Ma'am, is this girl staying here?"

She looked at the picture for a long minutes, then shook her head. "No. No, she ain't here."

"She's sixteen years old, but sometimes she dresses and makes herself up to look older. She may appear to be eighteen or nineteen, even twenty."

"No." She shook her head.

I pocketed the picture and turned to leave, disappointed. I had hoped that I would return to Baird triumphant and victorious, LeAnn Bertke in tow. "Well, thank you for your help."

"Not at all. If she comes in again, I'll let her know you were looking for her. Is there somewhere she should call?"

I stopped just as I reached the door. "Again"? Did she say "again"? I moved quickly back to the counter and placed the picture on it. "Ma'am, are you saying you know her?"

"Well, not by name or anything, but certainly I know her to talk to."

"How do you know her?" I asked.

"Oh, she's stayed here several times. Her and her brother. Nice kids. Stayed for a week. She'd come over and talk to me. Sometimes help me with the chores when her brother was out during the day. Said they was from Lexington, visiting folks hereabouts."

"What did her brother look like?" Naomi asked.

The motel lady squinched up her nose and thought for a moment. "Well, it's funny you should ask, because they didn't look at all like each other, you know? Not like most kin do. I mean, even kin who don't look alike, usually there's some family resemblance, around the eyes or the chin or something. But these two didn't look a thing alike."

"Can you remember the boy?"

"Well, I didn't see him as much as I saw the girl, you know, and it's been several months now, but let's see. . . ." She closed her eyes, and I could imagine her conjuring up a mental image. "He was about her age, maybe a little older. Tall and thin and blond with just a wisp of a mustache there. I don't think he was really old enough to have a mustache, if you know what I mean. It wasn't so much a mustache as some little blond hairs sorta growin' out under his nose." She giggled.

Naomi looked at me and sighed, then returned her attention to the old lady. "Did he wear a cap? Do you remember?"

"Why, yes, he did! With a funny thing on the front,

like a wishbone or something. Red it was, and flannel. Do you know him, miss?"

Naomi looked at me. "Adam," she said.

"Are you sure?" I said.

"It's a Cincinnati Reds cap. Authentic. Got it from one of the players at a game up in Cincinnati one time. He wears it everywhere. And the mustache."

"And the chin," said the motel lady. "Just a little dimple of a cleft in it. Like yours, miss."

Naomi looked at me and shrugged. Well, there you go.

"Do you remember when they were here?" I asked the motel lady.

"Well, right around Easter. Then once right after Christmas, and the first time was last fall. Three times in all, I believe. Such a sweet little thing. I hope nothing's happened to her."

"So do we," I said, and thanked her for her help.

"So now I guess you tell Ray, and Ray goes after Adam and picks him up for questioning," Naomi said as we drove back to town.

"I don't know. That sounds awful big-city cop to me. I can't see Ray picking anyone up for questioning. I think of him more as the having-a-talk-with kind of person," I said.

"It's not funny, Dan. Adam's my brother and I love him, and I don't want to see him get mixed up in anything like this. He wouldn't murder someone just for a piece of tail. Not when she was obviously giving it to him anyway."

I agreed with her that it seemed unlikely that Adam and LeAnn—two people whom I had never met—would kill the Martins for no apparent reason. The two young lovers seemed to have had all of the privacy and sexual experience they could handle at the Sawyer Motel.

On the other hand, I couldn't help wonder who was going to inherit the thirty thousand dollars from the Martins. If it was LeAnn Bertke, we might have another story altogether.

"You wanna try my cooking?" Naomi asked, bringing me out of my own thoughts. "I could cook us some supper when we get back."

"Thank you," I said. "But I have a sermon to finish, and Ray will want to know what I found out in town. Can I have a rain check?"

"How about lunch tomorrow after church?" she asked, not at all fazed by my rejection of her first offer.

"You're coming to church?"

She nodded. "Have to. You just made me a member of your parish, back there at that motel."

The motel! Jesus! What if someone saw us going in there together? Someone from the church? Didn't Naomi say that a lot of folks came to Perry on Saturday to shop? What if one of them . . .

No, I decided. That was just plain paranoid. Most of the people in Baird didn't even know me yet. Besides, the entrance to the motel office was away from the traffic. No one could have seen us from the road. But a little discretion would probably be in order in the future.

"Well," I said, trying to sound concerned, "usually some official committee or another wants to take the new pastor out to dinner or bring him home for chicken or something. It might not be politically wise to turn them down."

She laughed at that. "My, my, aren't we careful?

What are you, afraid someone will link us up together and have you married off before you're even settled in?"

I shrugged and tried a self-deprecating smile. It didn't feel as if it worked.

"I'll tell you what will happen," she said. "Ludene and Coletta Frank will invite you to their house for dinner so they can tell you what an asshole Donny Merriweather was, and the only reason they think that is because he didn't make a pass at them. And Haydon Smith will invite you over because his daughter is forty years old and still not married. And Verna and Tom Croozy will invite you over so they can tell you how sad they are at Donny's leaving and how you'll probably never measure up to him on accounta he burried their baby when it died in its crib last winter from sudden infant death syndrome and he kept them from going crazy from grief."

"You think?" I said, nearly laughing.

"I know," she said defiantly. "Now, which one of them is it that sounds so much better than having Sunday dinner with me?"

"I don't think your daddy likes me so much since he saw me with Ray Hall."

"What does Daddy have to do with this?" she asked.

"Well, I just thought that if I'm going to be eating at his table that I—"

"His table! I didn't invite you to Daddy's house. I invited you to mine. Now, are you comin' or aren't you?"

By this time we had driven to where my VW was parked and were sitting behind it at the curb. "You have a place of your own?" I asked.

"Prettiest view in the county," she said, smiling.

For a moment I thought about telling her that I had the prettiest view in the county at that very moment. But I didn't say it. No guts. What I did say was "Okay, it's a date. How do I find your place?"

"I'll pick you up after services," she said. "So keep the sermon short, okay?"

On the way home, I left the radio off and ran through my sermon in my mind. By the time I got to Baird, the sun was dropping behind Clark Mountain and I had managed to shave four minutes from my homily. My parishioners would never know what they'd missed.

Ray Hall, on the other hand, knew exactly what he had missed tromping all over Pine Tree Mountain looking for the missing LeAnn Bertke.

"Any luck?" I asked as I climbed out of the VW in front of the diner.

"Can a bear sing 'Dixie'?" he asked and flipped his cigarette butt a good twenty feet into the road. "Jesus Christ, what a waste of time."

I hoped my news from Perry would cheer him up at least a little.

Unlike Ray, I was not totally convinced that LeAnn wasn't up on Pine Tree Mountain somewhere, hiding or, worse, hidden by someone who didn't want her found. Maybe the same someone who killed the Martins. So Ray's bad news was my good news.

"Them damn dogs of Gilbert's ain't worth the powder it would take to blow their brains out. We walked all over that mountain, and all they found was a raccoon and three rabbits," he said, sitting down to a plate of beans and corn bread. He had taken a shower and changed his clothes, and his face was bright red from scrubbing. "Probably have poison ivy all over my sorry ass from this. And if I do, I'm gonna send the bill for my medicine to the good sheriff."

May June put a plate of beans and corn bread and a cold Budweiser in front of me. "You want onions, Dan?"

"Only if it's no trouble," I said to her.

"No trouble at all. The old man can't eat onions

anymore. They disagree with him. But I still chop 'em when I make beans. Habit, I guess."

Ray snorted. "She says onions make me fart. Can you figure that out? She feeds me a bowl of beans as big as a washtub and then blames the onions for making me fart." He shook his head at the mystery of feminine logic.

"Don't be crude, Dad," May June said. "Every time you eat onions you toss and turn all night long." She disappeared into the kitchen.

"So what'd you find out in Perry?" Ray asked me. He took a big gulp of beer and belched softly.

"The bodies will be released on Monday. Funeral will be Tuesday. I met LeRoy Whiteker."

"Boy who runs the funeral home?"

"Yeah. Nice guy."

"His daddy was a prick. Funny how that works out sometimes. Cause of death on the Martins?"

"No. Only an attendant at the morgue."

"I'll call on Monday. What else?"

"The Sawyer Motel was on target. That's where LeAnn Bertke was those three times she disappeared. It looks like she went there with Adam Taylor."

"For a whole week?"

"That's what the lady says. She said Adam would go off during the day and LeAnn would keep her company and help with chores." Not until I said it did it seem incongruous. "You know, Ray, LeAnn Bertke is turning out to be a complex kind of person."

Ray just nodded his head. He was breaking off little pieces of corn bread and chewing on them thoughtfully.

"It just doesn't sound like the same person, does it?" I continued. "One minute she's wearing peekaboo clothes and showing her breasts to the Carmack twins, and the next she's helping an old lady with her chores around a seedy motel. Does that make sense?"

Ray drank the rest of his beer and started his cigarette ritual. Finally, when he had the cigarette going, he leaned back in his chair and spoke. "People never make sense."

That was it.

And, when you think of it, it was all that needed to be said. Ray didn't make sense. He was smart and talented and could probably have done anything with his life that he wanted, and he'd chosen to stay in Baird and be the constable and postmaster.

I didn't make sense. I had thrown away what most ministers spend their entire lives trying to get, and all for roll on a desk top with a woman that, when I thought about it, I didn't like very much.

So why should anyone else, especially a sixteen-year-old girl who had been sexually abused by her crazy father and then carted off to an orphanage, be any more sensible than the two of us?

"I wonder what they were doing in that motel all week," Ray said.

"You're kidding, right?"

He looked at me without amusement. "For a whole week? No way. Not even a kid like Adam can keep it up nonstop for a whole week. Besides, you said he was gone during the day. I just wonder what he did while he was gone, is all."

"He probably went to work," I said. It seemed simple enough. "He didn't want anyone to get wise to his little rendezvous."

"Just didn't come home at night. That it?"

"He probably told his father he was with a friend or something."

Ray thought on it and nodded. "Maybe. I guess I'm gonna have to have a little talk with Adam whether he wants to talk or not."

"One other thing," I said, pushing my empty plate aside and taking out my pipe. "The Martins left an estate of thirty thousand dollars."

Ray blew out smoke and raised his eyebrows. "Well. That's enough money to kill for."

May June reentered from the kitchen carrying two enormous pieces of rhubarb pie in one hand and a coffee pot in the other. "Didja save room for dessert?" she asked us both.

Ray and I looked at each other and put down our smokes. The look on his face said, You don't turn down dessert from May June Hall and live to tell about it.

May June joined us for coffee, explaining that she had eaten with a couple of the girls earlier in the evening while they planned tomorrow's reception for the new pastor. Baking assignments had been made, and it was decided that the reception would be held in the basement of the church, as it was cooler than the backyard.

"Then you'll go to lunch at the Hazzards' place. John Hazzard is the chairman of the administrative board, and he'll want to fill you in on what all's going on in the church."

Oh, Lord. In my haste to accept Naomi's invitation to lunch I had forgotten that there might be someone with a legitimate claim on my time. I'd have to cancel. I hoped she would understand.

"Oops," I said, pushing my chair back. "I better make a quick call and cancel a conflicting lunch date."

"You got a lunch date for tomorrow?" May June said. "Not with Ludene and Coletta Frank, I hope. They're still mad about Don Merriweather not giving them a tumble."

"Why should he when they were giving it away for free?" Ray said, digging into his pie.

"You don't know that for a fact, old man," May June said over her shoulder. "You stay away from those two, Dan. They've been trouble for every minister that's come to this church. To hear them talk, they've bedded every pastor in the county."

"They must be something," I said.

"They're five feet tall, pug-nosed, and built like maple stumps," she responded bitterly. I was a little taken aback by the fire in her voice. "No one ever makes passes at them two, but that don't keep them from acting like it's so."

"And people believe them?"

"Never! It's just that it makes life miserable for the minister's all."

"Well," I said, rising, "I'm safe this time. My dinner date was with Naomi Taylor. I'll call her and take a rain check."

"No!" May June came out of her seat like a shot. "You've got a dinner date with Naomi Taylor? Really?"

I nodded.

She grabbed my arm and pushed me back into the chair. "Don't you dare miss that date. Why, Dan, she's the catch of the county. No man has been able to get even close to her, and many have tried."

Ray growled over his pie. "Her daddy cut their dicks off."

"Hush, now! You'll scare him off." Then to me, "We've been tryin' to get her hitched up for a long time. She's college educated, you know."

"So she tells me," I said.

"She went to U.T. Studied accounting or economics or finance or something. Graduated at the top of her class, then surprised everyone by building that little cabin up on the mountain and going to work for her daddy. We figured she was in for bigger things. Lexington, Cincinnati, maybe even Chicago."

"She's got a hot tub up there at that cabin," Ray said. He winked at me. "Sits out on the porch."

"Where are you taking her?" May June asked. "Somewhere nice, I hope."

"Well, I'm not exactly taking her anywhere. She invited me to her place."

May June nearly swooned. "Oh, my Lord. Do you know what that means?"

"She's a closet Methodist?"

Ray sputtered into his coffee and laughed out loud for what I presumed was the first time that day.

"No, silly," May June said, slapping Ray on his arm. "It means she likes you."

"You sound surprised," I said. "I'm really a pretty likable person, May June, once you get to know me."

"Oh, I know that. And you're handsome as the devil himself. It's just that, well, it's so exciting. Wait till I tell Dora and the girls. It'll be a scandal! The new divorced preacher comes to town and steals the heart of Naomi Taylor. It's just like one of those romance novels Dora's always reading."

"You tell Dora Musgrove and it'll be on the front

page of the *Herald* on Friday morning," Ray said, but he was smiling. " 'Methodist Minister Caught in Hot Tub with Baptist Hussy!' " He laughed.

I didn't. "May June, I really don't need a scandal in my life right now, if you know what I mean. Couldn't we be just a little bit discreet about this?"

"Oh, don't worry, Dan." She dismissed my concern with a flip of her hand. "He's just kidding. Everyone will be happy for you both."

"You sound like we're announcing our engagement," I said, not at all reassured. "I'm not so sure her father will find this luncheon so wonderful."

"Well, you're not eating it with him, are you? And his daughter is twenty-four years old and perfectly capable of doing as she darn well pleases." May June nodded her head once, and that was that.

"Yeah, fuck him," Ray said and chuckled as May June shook her head and fled from the room.

I went home excited about the prospect of my lunch with Naomi and worried about the fact that she was sixteen years younger than I was and the daughter of Hebrew Taylor. I couldn't concentrate on the sermon, so I hung my clerical robe in the bathroom and turned on the shower to steam the wrinkles out of it while I drank a diet Pepsi and changed the hymn numbers on the sign at the front of the sanctuary.

I tried to watch "Saturday Night Live," but the signal was so weak it was more trouble than it was worth. I'd have to talk to Ray about getting an antenna. Finally I gave up and went to bed and dreamed about Naomi Taylor.

She was hitchhiking and I offered to give her a ride and she offered to show me her breasts. That's what she called them, breasts. Not titties. But when I turned back to look at her—or her breasts, I'm not sure—she wasn't Naomi. She was LeAnn Bertke. I woke up with a raging erection and went back to sleep feeling guilty. But I slept well.

Sunday morning it was eighty degrees at eight o'clock, according to the R.C. Cola thermometer on my front porch, and the humidity was tropical. I ditched the idea of wearing a robe and got out my black suit. The clerical collar probably wouldn't do here, so I opted for a white shirt and a forgettable striped tie.

It was a good thing. The men in the congregation wore bib overalls with white shirts and ties, while the women wore housedresses with hats and gloves. High fashion was not the order of the day, and I was glad. Even with the windows open, the interior of the church hovered near ninety by the time services started at nine-thirty.

I introduced myself and thanked everyone for coming out on such a hot day. I announced the Martins' funeral on Tuesday morning and generally tried to be charming, but I had trouble keeping my mind on what I was doing, as Naomi had not appeared yet and I was beginning to think she had thought better of her offer.

Finally, having run out of charm, I announced the first hymn, Dora Musgrove (she of the gossipy tongue) played a flourish on the out-of-tune piano, and we were off. During the third verse of "Amazing Grace," Ray and May June entered the back of the church, and Naomi was with them. Ray winked, pointed at Naomi, shook his hand as though it had been burned, and mouthed the words, "Hubba-hubba."

May June whacked him on the arm and dragged him into a pew, but he had been right. Naomi was dressed in a lacy white dress that was at once absolutely virginal and overwhelmingly sexy. It was cut low in the front, but the lace covered her cleavage and the hem caught her at mid-knee. Her hair was down and shone in the sunlight that poured through the windows. She wore it in a simple pageboy style that framed her face without detracting from it. I caught my breath, felt my heart give an extra beat, and nearly fell out of the pulpit when she smiled at me and gave a little wave. I just smiled back and kept singing.

The service seemed to crawl like a turtle crossing a hot road. The prayers, the offering, the Scripture lesson, all floated by, and I got through it all. The sermon went well until someone said "Amen" out loud and I lost my train of thought for a moment. Had someone done that at my former church he would have been quietly asked to leave.

Well, maybe not, but it always seemed that way. Once I got used to it, though, I liked it. Every "Amen" gave me a little encouragement and confidence, and by the time it was over, I had preached one of my best sermons.

But then, sermons were the easy part. I was always good from the pulpit. It was in the office and the bedroom that I screwed things up—if you'll excuse the pun.

When the service ended, everyone was very happy, and I realized why when I looked at my watch and realized that it had only taken forty-five minutes. An hour is standard fare for most Methodists, and these folks seemed to like the abbreviated form, especially when the weather was so hot.

May June jumped up from her pew and ran to the front of the sanctuary during the last hymn, and after it was finished, she announced that the reception would be held in the basement. Coffee and cake were waiting for us there; cookies and punch were available for the kids in the yard behind the church.

I spent most of the reception sipping a diet Pepsi that I snagged from my own refrigerator before going downstairs, and desperately trying to remember names and faces.

Darnell Kody was dressed pretty much as he had been when I'd met him coming around the corner of the Mountain Baptist Children's Home carrying a gunnysack that turned out to be filled with snake. He was eating cookies whole, popping them into his mouth with his left hand. His right hand held what must have been a dozen more.

"Hey, Darnell," I said, offering my hand and then patting him on the arm as I noticed that both of his were busy.

"Hey, Reverent Dan," he said.

"Snakes keeping you busy?"

"Yeah." He giggled.

"You lose one recently?"

He rolled his eyes. "No." He giggled again and walked away, still stuffing cookies into his mouth.

"Darnell's not much on conversation," Jerry Sites said from beside me. He was drinking a cup of red punch.

"I guess not," I said. "How's he doing with the snakes under the porch?"

"He got 'em out yesterday," Jerry said, shaking his head. "I don't know how he did it, and to tell you the truth I don't really care. Damned things give me the creeps. I can't say's I can blame Rachael for how she reacted the other night at your place." He took a sip of his punch and then looked up suddenly at me. "Hey, you don't think ol' Darnell had anything to do with that—"

I cut him off with a shake of my head. "No. I was just wondering if anyone else in town knew there was a free supply of snakes under your porch."

"Well, probably everyone in town knew about 'em. Ol' Darnell doesn't exactly keep things like that a secret. But it wasn't him. I'd stake my life on that." He finished his punch and looked around for a place to set his cup. Finding none, he shifted it from one hand to the other. "You find out any more about the Martins?"

"Nothing that can help. Ray's still following up on LeAnn Bertke. Trying to find her. But who knows?"

Jerry shook his head and fumbled with his empty punch cup. "It really is a shame. Mac and Ernie were really fine people. Helped us at the home any time we needed it."

"Everyone I've talked to seems to say the same thing. The community's going to miss them. I wish I'd had the chance to know them."

"I guess smoke inhalation probably did it. I suppose we can take some comfort in the fact that Ernie probably never felt a thing. Just slept through the whole thing." He slapped his thigh and shook his head. "Damn! Why'd he have to go back into the house? Mac was a smart man, Dan. I just can't believe he'd run back into a burning house."

"He loved his wife," I said. Somehow that seemed like reason enough to me.

"I love my wife, but ... I don't know if I could be

that brave." He looked into his empty cup and shook his head. "Well, I guess I better mingle a bit. Good luck." And he was gone. Mingling, talking, laughing, and always with just a hint of worry in his eyes. I wondered who would take the place of the Martins at the children's home. Folks like that don't come around very often.

The Carmack twins were there with their wives, who were nowhere near as homely as the boys. Plump, pleasant women who talked a mile a minute and, no doubt, ran the church.

After about half an hour Ray slipped up beside me, eating a piece of white cake as big as my VW.

"You wanna come with me tomorrow morning to talk to Adam Taylor? I figure you got a right," he said, shoveling cake into his mouth with a plastic fork.

"How do you figure, Ray?" I asked, smiling and shaking hands with people. "You're the law. I was just helping out yesterday, since I had to go to town anyway."

"You had the snake in your kitchen," he said.

"Do you think Adam had something to do with that?"

Ray shrugged his shoulders. "Could be."

I thought about it for a few seconds but decided against it. "I really need to start being a pastor here. I have the Martins' funeral to prepare, and I probably ought to call on some folks tomorrow. They'll be expecting it, especially since I can't go to dinner with them today."

Ray nodded. "Fine. You're probably right. Just thought I'd extend the invitation's all."

I thanked him, and he strolled away, nodding to

folks and talking with others, perfectly at ease. A big fish in a small pond.

"You wanna change clothes before we leave?" Naomi said from beside me.

"You like sneaking up on me?" I asked. "You did that yesterday."

"I like the way you look at me when I catch you off guard."

"The way I look at you?" Just about everyone had shaken hands by now, and they were attacking the cake in full force. I turned to look at her straight on.

"Yeah," she said. "Most guys around here, all they can see is big boobs and straight teeth. They look at me and they think, bed."

"And I'm different?" I asked, thinking that I wasn't much, if at all.

"Well, sorta. I mean, you like what you see and all, but it isn't just lust. It's more like, I don't know, appreciation, I guess."

I didn't know what to say to that, so I said, "I very much appreciate your coming over today."

"My pleasure," she said, smiling. "You're good, you know. How'd you wind up here?"

"What's wrong with here? Baird, Kentucky, doesn't deserve a good pastor?" I asked, maybe a little too defensively.

But she just smiled and let her eyes take in the basement of the church. "Well, it ain't no crystal cathedral."

"And I ain't no Robert Schuller," I said, smiling. "Let me thank May June and the girls and change clothes and I'll be ready to go. What should I wear?"

"Sloppies," she said. "Whatever's comfortable. We'll do some walking, maybe."

I said fine, found May June in the little church kitchen cutting another cake, and said I was going. She took my hand and squeezed it and said, "You go on and don't worry about a thing here." Then she winked at me, and for a moment she looked just like Ray.

"I'll expect a full report when you get back," she said as I walked out of the kitchen.

The view from Naomi Taylor's balcony was indeed the best in the county.

The cabin itself snuggled into the side of Mount Devoux, the third of Baird's guardian mountains, about ten miles from the church. The balcony stood on stilts and hung precariously off the side of the mountain. Beyond, the Appalachians rolled in twenty shades of green, lapping over and over each other in what seemed like an infinite progression. Small clouds lodged themselves into the valleys and gave the view greater depth and an almost unnatural dimension. It was a picture postcard, but the view didn't come cheap.

The ten-mile drive had taken close to forty minutes, winding and twisting up the side of the mountain on a road that left no room for error—a wall of sandstone and pine forest on the right, hundred-foot valleys on the left. About every half mile or so a rusted derelict pickup truck or car could be seen at the bottom of the valley, evidence of some poor soul's lack of brakes or driving skill. Or both.

Naomi parked the car on a small apron next to the road, and we had to hike nearly a half mile into the woods and up the mountain to get to the cabin. I wondered what it must be like to lug groceries that far two or three times a week, or even to get the mail, for that matter.

We approached the cabin from the rear and entered a mud room and then a kitchen that was small but extremely well ordered, perfect for one cook and no more.

At the other end of the kitchen was a breakfast bar, on the other side of which was the living-dining room, paneled in knotty pine, extending to a wall of glass and the breathtaking view of the mountains. The fireplace was as big as most closets, and pegs on the walls held hats, coats, and even chairs. Antique photographs and tintypes, shelves overflowing with paperback books, and some overstuffed furniture, built for comfort rather than speed, all joined together in a symphony of coziness.

I couldn't hear the air conditioner, but the cabin was comfortably cool. Down a small hall were a bedroom, a small office, and a bathroom in which all the normal stuff had apparently been hastily dumped into a drawer and the new towels brought out.

The place had a new but comfortable feel to it, as though it had not taken the occupant long to make it into a home.

"My brothers and Dad built it," she said as we finished the tour. "It was my price for coming back here after college."

"You can be bought?" I asked, smiling.

"Only with money," she said. "And a great house. You hungry?"

I had eaten a piece of cake at the reception, so the hunger that normally attacks at noon was still at least an hour away. She said, fine, she would put the chicken in the fridge, change her clothes, and we could take a walk.

When I think of taking a walk, what comes to mind is a stroll down the street to the ice cream shop that stood at the end of my block in Louisville, a double dip of cherry cordial, and a slow stroll back to my apartment. What we did that Sunday was more like a hike than any walk I had ever taken.

I had worn an old pair of khaki walking shorts and a golf shirt, athletic socks, and running shoes. Naomi emerged from her bedroom in a pair of cutoffs identical to the ones I had first seen her in, high-top basketball shoes, and a T-shirt with "Gatlinburg!" scrolled across the breast. Her hair was pulled back in the same George-style ponytail that I had seen at her father's house. She looked great.

We hiked downhill most of the time, on a trail that I could just barely make out but Naomi seemed to be completely familiar with. The temperature hovered near one hundred, and the humidity in the woods was nearly that, so we took our time. Both of us sweated freely, and we stopped frequently to drink from a canteen she had filled at the cabin and to swat away gnats and mosquitoes.

As we walked, she told me about college and coming home to work for her dad. "Not because he really needs me but because he's dying. I won't have the chance to work for him long, but what I can give him, I do. I owe him that much."

Since her return to Baird she had computerized all of the old man's bookkeeping and financial records from the old bound volumes he had kept all of his life. That done, the work took only ten or twelve hours a week. The rest of the time she spent hiking, fixing up her house, reading, or cooking for her father and brothers, the youngest of whom was five-year-old Isaiah.

Naomi was the daughter of Mary Lee Taylor, Hebrew's second wife, who had died of cancer when Naomi was eight years old. Hebrew had married again, of course, and Lucy B. Taylor had walked out after giving him Isaiah. The total for Hebrew Taylor was now three wives, seven children, four businesses, all of Clark Mountain. And not one bit of it could save him from the disease that was turning his lungs to stone.

Naomi had three older brothers and three younger. She didn't differentiate between brothers and half brothers, she said, because none of the mothers were around or alive and Daddy was, and he was all that counted.

For my part, I told her how I came to be the pastor of the Baird Methodist Church. I told her the whole story—the *Reader's Digest* version—much as I have told it to you, and her response was what I might have expected but didn't.

"So are you gun-shy now about women in your parish?" she said, pushing aside a branch and holding it down until I could get past.

"I don't know," I said honestly. "This is my first parish since the big fall, and I haven't had the chance to find out yet."

"What about in Louisville, while you were teaching?"

"I was a monk. I lived in a one-room apartment, taught, graded papers, cooked, and slept. On weekends I worked out in a local gym and read."

"Whoa!"

"It wasn't bad, really. Kind of peaceful. But . . ."

"But a person can do only so much penance."

I shrugged. "I guess so."

The trail suddenly ended, and we were at the top of a cliff that looked out over an impossibly blue lake, maybe a hundred feet down. The cliff and the opposite shore were reflected perfectly in the calm water, and the scene was more beautiful than it had any right to be.

At one end of the lake a rock wall stairway stepped up from the water to about the same level as we were standing at. At the other end, at the same level as the water, were some run-down shacks and a small beach.

"The Viper Quarry," she said.

"It's beautiful." We sat and dangled our legs over the edge and drank from the canteen. I took out my pipe and worked hard to get it going. The matches from my shirt pocket were sweat-soaked, but the ones in my pants pocket were salvageable.

"About fifty years ago they discovered limestone here and they went in to get it. Took them about fifteen years to dig it out. Lots of jobs. Baird was a boomtown. Then one day the usable limestone ran out, and the company vanished."

"And so did the jobs," I said. I was just starting to feel the little rush I get when I first light a pipe, and I enjoyed it.

"That's right. The town of Viper, right down that

road there, went bust. It's a ghost town now except for the store, and all she sells is pop and cigarettes, when she decides to open." She sighed. "Pretty, though, isn't it?"

"Any fish?"

"No. Too many chemicals. I'm not sure what. See how blue the water is? How clear? It's not natural. The lake should be full of algae, but the chemicals won't let it grow, so it's just a big empty hole filled with water."

"How deep is it?"

She shrugged. "Daddy used to tell us it was bottomless so we'd get scared and not go swimming in it. Maybe a hundred feet in some places."

I blew out smoke with a woosh. "That's deep!"

We sat there saying nothing. After a few minutes she sighed and leaned against me, and I let my right arm go around her and rest across her back. Neither of us was concerned about perspiration. After a while the name of the place struck me as odd.

"How did it get its name?"

"You mean 'Viper'?"

I nodded.

"The quarry or the town?" she asked.

"Either one. Whichever came first."

"Well, the quarry came first. The town went up because of the quarry. Not much of a town, really. Filling station, couple of stores, couple of restaurants, little Pentecostal church. Most of it for the quarry workers."

"Why 'Viper'?" I asked, coming back to the subject.

She sat up away from me and looked intently at the lake, thinking. "It was because of the snakes," she said at length.

"The snakes?"

"Yeah. On the steps yonder." She pointed at the far end of the lake, where the wall was terraced down to the edge of the water. "For some reason, when they first started cutting into the mountain like that it attracted snakes. One day they'd cut a shelf into the mountain, and the next day they'd come back and find snakes sunning themselves out on the rock, there. Hundreds of them, they say. I wasn't even born yet when this happened, so it's just what I heard."

"What kind of snakes?" I asked.

"All kinds, I guess. Why?"

"Just curious. It's a weird name."

She tilted her head in thought. "Yeah, I guess it is. Funny, I never thought of it before. It was always just there, you know. The Viper Quarry. I never gave much thought to the name."

"What happened to the snakes?" I asked.

"Well, they say that they had to kill 'em and clean 'em up every day for a while, and then one day they just stopped being there. Funny, huh?"

"Yeah. Funny." But in truth, since the night with Rachael Sites, I found nothing funny about snakes. Nothing funny at all. I shivered at the thought of the hundreds that must have covered the terraced wall at the end of the lake.

Naomi stood and dusted off her butt with her hands. "Well, ready to start back?"

I was and we did.

Did I mention that most of the trip to Viper Quarry had been downhill? So of course the trip back to the cabin was uphill.

Dear God, in that heat and humidity. We stopped

every fifteen minutes or so to catch our breath and take a sip of water, and even at that I thought I might die from the effort. I took some little comfort in the fact that Naomi, more than ten years my junior and in considerably better shape than I was, seemed to be having her own problems.

An hour and a half later, wheezing and coughing, soaked to the skin with perspiration, legs weak and trembling, we stumbled into the little yard around the cabin and collapsed. While I tried to catch my breath and vowed for the thousandth time to give up my pipe, Naomi disappeared into the cabin and then reappeared with two cold beers.

"I set the chicken out and I put a couple more of these in the freezer," she said. "I don't guess you're hungry just now?"

My breathing was still too labored to talk. I shook my head, pressed the cold can against my temple, and leaned forward, my head between my raised knees. My chest was finally beginning to recover. At least it didn't feel as if it was going to implode anymore.

"Here," she said, handing me a big white towel. "Ray probably told you about the hot tub."

"I figured it was a figment of his imagination, or wishful thinking," I gasped. "He said it was on the balcony."

"No, it's under the balcony. I built a cozy for it, open only on the side facing the view. There's a door in the cozy so you can get in and out." She stood and pointed the way. "Just leave your clothes on the steps outside the door. I'll throw them in the wash, and they can dry while we eat."

"And, uh, what will I wear while my clothes dry?" I asked, smiling but serious.

"I've got one of daddy's robes in my room. Sometimes he comes over and sits in the tub. He says the steam helps his breathing." She shook her head, and sweat flew from the ends of her hair. "I think he just likes to feel decadent. I told him to buy one for himself, but he said it'd just be a waste of money on someone as old as him."

I nodded. I had a mother who was not unlike Naomi's father in many ways.

"I keep the water cool in the summer, so don't worry about him showing up for steam therapy," she said, reading the worried expression on my face. "And no one will see you. You can't get more private than this."

Well, what the heck. It had been a hell of a week, and we preachers aren't above a little decadence when the occasion presents itself. Naomi gave me the rest of her beer and told me to enjoy myself; she would hang the robe on the doorknob and call me when supper was ready.

Dare I saw "heaven"? For that is what the hot tub was.

The water was not cold. Just nice and cool, the bubbles and whirlpools eddying around my back and legs, massaging and relaxing every part of my body. I ducked my head under several times, tried to fix my hair with my fingers, and then let it go. Hebrew Taylor had probably left an extra comb around here somewhere as well as a robe.

I finished my beer and started on Naomi's, which was getting warm, but I didn't care. I could have lain that way for a long, long time and not cared about anything. The view, the beer, the tub, the girl . . .

Dear Lord, it was wonderful.

"How ya doing?" she said from the other side of the door.

I roused myself from a near-snooze. "Wonderfully," I called back. "How about you?"

"Can't complain. I have a confession to make, though."

"Whatever it is, you're absolved. Go and sin no more."

"Don't you even want to hear what it is?" she asked, giggling.

"Nope." I felt that good.

"You sure?"

"Oh, okay. Confess your sins if it will make you feel any better."

The door opened, and she stood at the top of the steps, her bare feet level with the edge of the tub. She was wearing a white robe, and her hair was pulled up on top of her head. "I don't really have one of Daddy's robes here," she said, smiling.

For just a split second a wisp of worry, of concern, found its way into my mind, and then it was gone just as quickly as it had come. I felt the hunger that was left after two years of celibacy, I weighed the possible consequences of what seemed to be happening, I decided I didn't give a damn, and I said, "Oh."

I have never claimed to be a smooth talker anywhere but in the pulpit. And this was certainly not a pulpit. Nowhere near a pulpit.

She let the robe slip off her shoulders, tossed it to the steps behind her, and walked, gracefully naked, down into the tub. When she was thigh deep, she turned and lifted two more beers from the steps behind her. "Do you feel seduced?" she said, sitting on the edge of the tub.

"A little," I said. I just sat there like an idiot, taking in her perfect body. The beautiful face, the marvelous breasts, not overly large but firm, the nipples pointing slightly up. Tight stomach, slight flare of her hips, and well muscled but supple legs. Jesus, she was a vision. "But I don't mind. Do you mind being stared at?"

"No. Remember what I said? I like the way you look at me."

"Well, I like to look. So that should make both of us happy." I felt my face smile. The beer was having a great effect. I wondered briefly what the smile looked like, but she smiled back, so I stopped caring.

She sat the beers on the edge of the tub and leaned back, arching her back and stretching. Then, looking into my eyes, she parted her legs ever so slightly, scooped up water with her hand, and let it dribble down her belly.

I felt my groin tighten and harden, come to attention, and I figured that watching time was over. Somehow she seemed to read my mind and came to me, her arms going around my head and her breasts to my face.

I kissed and sucked her nipples and let my hands decide on their own course, searching, exploring, probing every inch of her body. She reached between my legs and stroked me gently and moaned deep in her throat so that I could feel the vibrations against my face.

Like dancers, our bodies began to respond with greater urgency, molding themselves together in passion. Our petting and groaning became more frantic. We kissed, and each kiss was deeper and more searching than the one before.

Slowly she eased herself down onto me, and we

began to make slow, graceful love, sloshing the water gently over the edge of the tub. Her breasts brushed against my chest, and I cupped her hips in my hands. After a few minutes our movements became more defined, the thrusting more powerful, longer, deeper, until great tidal waves were crashing back and forth across the pool. She grabbed the back of my head and pressed my face firmly against her breasts, leaned back, taking me with her, cried out, and shuddered. I continued to make love to her and, in a moment, joined her in climax.

We did not separate immediately, but stayed that way, her sitting on my lap, facing me, legs on either side, joined intimately, for what seemed like a long time. She stroked my hair and I rubbed her back. She kissed my neck and ear, and I ran my hands over her hips and stroked her gently where we were joined.

That gentle afterglow was a wonderful, peaceful place to be. Like the cabin itself. A place to hide away and see only beauty and joy. Here, in this place, you could get away from the poverty, the cruelty, the snakes, if only for a moment, and see only beauty and feel good. I did not want to leave it.

And then, out of nowhere, I thought of Ray Hall, and I started laughing. It was awful timing, I know, but what can I say? Maybe it was the beer. Maybe it was two years of celibacy. Maybe it was just the sheer joy of the whole day. But I started to laugh, and I couldn't stop.

"What?" Naomi said, leaning back and looking at me in surprise. "What, Dan?"

"Ray!"

"Ray Hall? What about him?"

I laughed on, tears beginning to stream down my

face, my stomach cramping from the effort. "What he said!"

She started to laugh now. "What? What did he say?"

"He said ... Oh, God, it's not that funny. ... It's just such a great day, and ..."

She did something with her hips that took my breath away and brought me back to attention. "Tell me!" she said, now laughing nearly as hard as I was.

"Oh, God, that's good!" I laughed on. "Do that again. I may never tell you if you keep torturing me like that."

"Dan, for God's sake ... tell me what he said."

I swallowed and took a breath and blurted it out as fast as I could before the laughter came back. "It was a newspaper headline he said would be in the *Herald* ... oh, God ... if anyone found out about me coming up here. He said, 'Methodist Minister Caught in Hot Tub with Baptist Hussy.' " I continued to laugh.

For a second she sat there thinking about it; then she, too, exploded in laughter. We giggled our way through the two beers and then continued the party on a blanket on the thick carpet of the air-conditioned living room, watching dirty movies on her TV, eating cold chicken, drinking beer, and making love.

We did not walk down the hill to the car until nearly 11:00 P.M. Hey, two years is a long time.

14

"What is it?" she asked, as I steered her LTD down the mountain.

"Just thinking," I answered.

"What are you thinking about?"

"Oh, you."

"The Baptist hussy who will be your downfall?"

All I could do was smile. I didn't want to say it. It felt stupid and unreasonable, but it was still there. Two years ago I had lost my whole life because of a stupid sexual urge. Something down inside me kept whispering, "Are you doing it again?" It sounded a little like my mother's voice.

"That is it, isn't it?" she said. "I don't believe it."

"I'm sorry. It's just that ... I don't know." The thoughts were making me feel bad, and having the thoughts was making me feel bad. Being with her in the cool, hidden interior of the cabin had been like being in another world—safe, exciting, forbidden, and altogether wonderful. Now I was driving back to the real world where they hung ministers out to dry who ventured into that other world where men and women made love with wild abandon in a mountainside hot tub. "It just seems too good to be true. I mean, why me? Jesus, you've only known me three days."

She leaned back in her seat and covered her eyes with her hands. "Oh, my God! Men! You think you're the only ones who have sexual feelings. You're a chauvinist, Reverend Thompson!"

"Naomi, I'm sorry. I didn't mean—"

"Let me tell you something. Durel County is hardly a hot bed of eligible bachelors on the upward track, you know? Most of the women here get married right out of high school, have babies, and spend their lives cooking grits and changing diapers. And that's exactly the way the men want it!

"Well, I don't want that. I want something more out of life. But my father's dying, and I decided to spend the last couple of years he has left helping him out. So I put myself right in the middle of Appalachia to do it. What do you think, that you're the only one who's lived like a monk the last two years?

"Turn here, I'll show you Viper. It's a ghost town now, as I said before, but kind of interesting. The road comes back out about three miles down the mountain."

I followed her instructions and made a right turn onto a narrow paved road, almost overgrown on both sides. I dropped my speed immediately to about twenty miles per hour.

"Anyway," she continued, picking up her recitation where she'd left off. "Here I am, living in an intellectual wasteland because I love my father, and the only men around are unemployed, uneducated, unattractive, married, or all four.

"Then one day I get introduced to the new Methodist minister. He's handsome, he's educated, and he looks at me as if he's just witnessed the Second Coming—all of which is just fine with me, even if he is a little old for me."

"I'm not that old," I interrupted.

"Don't interrupt. So I try a couple of things there in the front yard of Daddy's house while you're sitting in the Jeep with Ray, figuring it's safe because Ray's there. You know, wiggle my butt, flirt, play the bitch goddess.

"But I realize that this new preacher's not into games and if I keep it up I may scare him off. So when I meet him in town by coincidence on Saturday I try being nice, and, what do you know? It works. He's nice, too. So I invite him to Sunday dinner, as any self-respecting Christian girl would. I figure, hey, cold chicken, some nice intellectual conversation like I haven't had in two years since I left U.T. It would be great!

"Then I go to church to be supportive and nice again, and I hear him preach. And, God! This guy can preach! He really believes what he's saying."

"I do believe it, you know," I said, feeling somehow defensive.

"I know you do! God, Jesus Christ, grace, love, forgiveness, mercy, justice. You believe! And everyone in that church can see it, and it's like it's the first time any of them have ever heard any of it, even though they've been going to church all their lives. It's like, I don't know, magic or something.

"And right there I feel my stomach roll over and

my heart kind of lurch in my chest, and I say to myself, 'My God, look at them. Every woman in this church is in love with him.' And they were! And I figure, girl, if you think you want him, you better make your move fast, or someone else will."

I didn't know what to say. I'd never really experienced worship from the other side of the pulpit. Even when I sat in a pew for two years and watched, I always imagined myself up there in front. I didn't listen to the sermons so much as critique them.

"So I decided to make my move. I didn't know what I was going to do, but I knew I'd do something. And I knew that you didn't play games. Nothing subtle would work."

She looked out the window, and I saw her wipe a tear from her cheek. "That's Viper up there," she said.

We drove through the town in slow silence. The one streetlight threw a gray cast on the store, which was closed up tight. The old Pentecostal church was still standing, barely. The two restaurants and the bar were nearly falling down. They had been boarded up long ago and left to rot. Of the other buildings, only the foundations and a couple of chimneys still visible, the wood having fallen away. The entrance to the quarry was blocked with a sawhorse and a chain. A No Trespassing sign hung from the sawhorse.

I saw little of this, so caught up was I in Naomi's version of the last three days. It had never occurred to me to see it from her point of view. All I could think of was myself, what I was doing, what she was doing to me, what effect it would have on me. I felt like a heel, but I didn't know what to say. I tried to think how I would counsel a person in my position. What would I advise him to say? Everything I thought of sounded trite and silly. Finally I pulled over to the side of the road in front of one of the boarded-up buildings and fell back on the old and familiar.

"I'm sorry, Naomi," I said, and tried to make it sound sincere. "I guess I'm still a little gun-shy. Not many good things have happened to me in the past two years, and I tend not to trust the ones that do happen."

She was crying. Not out loud or openly, but I could tell from her breathing. "I was so scared," she said after a few minutes. "I wanted to hold your hand or have you put your arm around me. I wanted to walk close to you and brush up against you and smell your cologne, and all I could think was 'What if he brushes you off because you're so young? What if he laughs at you? You're just a silly little twit with a crush on your minister!' I just kept thinking those things.

"Even in the hot tub, when I first came through the door, I was so scared when I took the robe off my legs were shaking. That's why I got down in the tub so quick. That's why I gave you all that beer."

"You were scared?" It was hard to believe. But then, the truly perfect are never aware of their own perfection. Probably the same holds true for the truly beautiful. "I thought I'd have a heart attack right there in the tub," I said. "I was terrified. Here's this beautiful young woman who can hike my ass off and can have any man in the state of Kentucky, and for some reason she wants me?"

"I do want you, Dan. But I'm not that woman in your office. I won't ruin your life if I can't have you. I won't make a fool of myself following you around and ruining your career. I don't have to do that. I've got too much going for me, and the world's too big a place to die here over one man, no matter how great I think he is."

She wasn't crying anymore. She was looking straight ahead, her arms folded across her chest. I started the car and eased back onto the road, feeling like a shit.

"Naomi, I can't even begin to tell you how great this day has been for me. How great you've been for me. I hope I haven't blown the whole thing by being such a thickheaded chauvinist. I guess what I'm saying is that as great as today was, I want to try some of that intellectual conversation before we slip on the wedding bands."

She turned to me, and her expression softened just a little. "You city boys are so slow-movin'. Up here in the mountains, you see what you want, you claim it and fast."

"Before someone else does," I said, smiling.

She smiled and started to say something, and the rear window exploded, showering us with glass.

Naomi screamed and threw her hands up behind her head as I slammed on the brakes and sent the LTD into a sideways skid that threatened to send us off the road into a ditch or a tree.

Another explosion and the driver's-side window cracked and spiderwebbed around a neat hole, the twin of which appeared almost simultaneously in the passenger-side window.

"Get down!" I screamed at Naomi, steering like a madman, trying to get the car going straight down the road again.

"What is it? What's happening?" she shouted as she tried to crouch down in the front seat.

I lowered my head as far as I could and still see

over the steering wheel. "Someone's shooting at us!"
I said.

"Who? Why?"

I clicked on the bright lights and pressed the accelerator. The speedometer began to creep up toward fifty. "I don't know," I said, steering like crazy, my hands gripping the wheel too tight. "Trespassing?"

"It's a ghost town!" she said. She poked her head up to try to look over the seat back.

"Stay down, dammit!" I shouted, and she dropped back down behind the seat.

I hit the turnoff where the Viper cutoff rejoined the main road at fifty-five miles per hour and almost lost it on the turn. The rear end fishtailed again, and it felt as if the car might go over, but I managed to correct it at the last minute and get us going back down the mountain toward Baird.

The main road was dark and seemed quiet enough, so I brought the speed back down to a reasonable thirty-five, sighed, and loosened my grip on the wheel. My hands ached with the effort and took a few seconds to open. They felt cold and clammy.

Two headlights appeared in the rearview mirror, and I felt a little better. We were clear of Viper with its mad gunman, and with another car on the road, it was unlikely that anyone would try to attack both of us.

Naomi eased herself back to a sitting position and brushed the glass off her shoulders. She reached across to my shoulders and brushed the glass away, briskly flipping it into the backseat, and her eyes shot open. "Oh, my God. You're bleeding!"

For the first time, I felt the blood trickling down the back of my shirt and an incredible itching on the back of my neck. "Glass," I said. "I can feel it in my neck."

"Slow down a little," she said, getting up on her knees in the seat and leaning toward me. "Let that car's lights get a little closer and I'll be able to see how bad it is. Give me your hanky."

I slowed, but not too much. I didn't want the other vehicle to pass me on that narrow road and leave us alone again in the dark. Naomi began to pick shards of glass out of my neck and dab at the blood with my handkerchief.

"I think I can get most of it," she said. "We'll have May June look at it when we get back. She's kind of the Granny woman for this area."

"Granny woman?" I said. My neck was beginning to hurt now, but Naomi's hands were gentle and I liked being cared for. The car behind us got a little too close, so I took the LTD up to forty.

"Medicine woman," she said. "A granny woman is like a cross between a midwife and a medicine man. She knows first aid, birthing, and some herbal remedies. Actually, I think May June reads about some of that stuff, too."

The car behind us sped up again and looked as if it was going to crowd past us on the right, so I slowed down and didn't try to prevent it. Naomi was almost finished with my neck, and I figured that we were far enough from Viper to be safe. If I remembered the road correctly, we would be back in Baird in fifteen or twenty minutes.

"Well, I think that's the best I can do," Naomi said.

The car started to pass us, and I pulled as far to the right as I could to let it go by.

It rammed us from the rear before Naomi could sit

back down, and she bounced against the seat and then up against the windshield. I heard her head hit the glass and saw the windshield crack in five different directions. She sank to the floor with a little whimper, and the LTD slewed to the left, across the road.

Another crash and the steering wheel was ripped out of my hands and the car started to zigzag crazily all over the road. We hadn't left the danger in Viper at all, I realized. It had followed us out onto the main road and was trying to run us off the mountain.

I grabbed the steering wheel with all the strength I could manage, and my neck screamed as I tightened my grip.

Another crash hit the back of the car, but this time I held it tight, and we shot out a good fifty feet in front of our pursuers. I tromped on the accelerator, and the speedometer shot up to sixty.

The trees became a blur, and I tried not to think of the sheer drop on the right-hand side where I had seen the hulks of other cars rusting at the bottom on our way up the mountain.

The headlights of the other car receded to two small dots in the rearview mirror, and I eased up on the gas. Surely they weren't crazy enough to drive this fast on such a dangerous road.

Then the lights started getting bigger, and I remembered the coal trucks screaming down the mountain. They were familiar with these roads. They knew every twist and turn. Sixty miles per hour was cruising speed for them.

They were gaining on me, and I couldn't drive any faster. My arms began to ache with the strain of holding the wheel, and my neck was bleeding again. I could feel the blood running freely down my back, and my stomach started to turn over. My ears began to ring.

Oh, Christ! Not now! You can't faint, I told myself. Get a grip! Come on, think of something!

I couldn't get out and run. Naomi was out cold, probably with a concussion, and this was a mountain road. Sheer cliffs on both sides. Up on the left, down on the right.

Turn and fight? Maybe. I'd seen a movie once where a guy did that or, rather, made it look as if he was doing that. He got his family out of the car, swung it around to face the oncoming car, and turned the lights on bright, then jumped out and left the car sitting on a bridge. The bad guys thought he was playing chicken and didn't realize until it was too late that the car was empty. They died in a fiery crash.

All of this took maybe two seconds to run through my mind, and I rejected the idea in even less time. No bridge. No place to run.

In those two seconds the car behind us had gained and was no more than thirty feet away.

I took my foot off the accelerator and let them come up another twenty feet. If they hit me again I didn't want to be going sixty miles per hour. My speed dropped to fifty and they came on, ten feet off my bumper.

This was it, then. I braced myself for another crash and stared hard at the road.

A little green sign flashed by: S.R. 42—One Mile. Route 42 was the main road that went through Baird and on to Perry. One mile and I could turn left and be four straight safe miles from Baird. One more lousy mile. I glanced at the odometer.

The crash came, just as I was expecting, only this

time I didn't accelerate. I braked just enough to keep my bumper against theirs.

Eight-tenths of a mile to Baird.

I heard them gun their engine and felt the LTD start to lurch forward and thought for a moment I had made a bad mistake. The vehicle behind us was a pickup truck, only a half-ton job, but big enough to bulldoze us right off the road. I pressed harder on the brake, the LTD's wheels slowed, and the brakes squealed under the pressure.

Six-tenths of a mile.

Our forward progress slowed, but we were still moving slowly toward the edge of the road, toward the drop-off. I pushed the brakes to the floor, the wheels locked, and we began to grind to a stop. The smell of burning rubber floated through the car.

Three-tenths of a mile.

At walking speed and slower we eased down the last part of the mountain road as it began to level out. I said a quick prayer, rolled down my window, letting pieces of glass fall in my lap, and listened intently.

The bumpers were clunking together and the tires were still squealing, but over it I heard the sound I had prayed to hear. A quick thud and a grinding of gears. Trust these good old boys to have a stick shift. The driver was downshifting. I felt like screaming in triumph as I tromped the big Ford's accelerator to the floor and shot away from him like a bullet.

As soon as the truck lurched forward without pursuing us, I knew I had him. I screeched to a halt and flew backwards, driving with my left hand, my neck screaming as I tried to look out the nonexistent back window.

He had stalled the truck in his rush to chase us, and

I intended to stall him permanently if possible. I hit his front bumper with the rear of the LTD, and the impact carried us right up over the bumper into the grill, radiator, and fan of the truck.

There was a deafening crash, the scream of grinding metal, and I said another quick prayer that I hadn't gotten locked on his bumper. I needn't have bothered with the prayer. The truck rolled back, and the LTD dropped free. The trunk of the old Ford was pushed up and back into the backseat, and the hood of the pickup had popped open. Gray steam billowed out of the engine and formed a giant cloud in the road. I shifted gears and shot forward again.

I hit State Route 42 like a pro, controlled the skid, and flew toward Baird going seventy miles per hour. All the way, I talked to Naomi and tried to get her to respond, but she said nothing. I pounded the dash with my fist and cut it on the glass there. I screamed and swore at her, pleaded and begged her to wake up. Nothing.

When I saw the lights of Baird, I pressed down on the horn and didn't let up until I skidded to a stop beside Ray's Jeep in front of the Baird Store and Diner.

15

"You look like death warmed over," Ray said. "Mother, quick, get him some coffee."

I walked into the diner, sat on a stool next to Ray, and May June sloshed a big mug before me. "Breakfast?" she asked. I nodded and held my thumb and forefinger a half inch apart. Just a little. She started buttering two pieces of Wonder bread for the griddle.

The coffee made me feel human again, but my neck and head still throbbed. I asked May June for the bottle of aspirin sitting above the stove, and she handed it over. I washed four of them down with another gulp of coffee and decided I might be able to talk.

"How's Naomi?" I asked. The whole back of my head ached with the effort, but until I found out about Naomi I could think of little else.

Ray and May June had heard me coming the night before and yanked the doors of the car open before the engine had died.

Ray pulled me out and helped me to the porch and into a rocker while May June looked over Naomi. I tried to tell Ray what had happened, but he was gone before I could collect my thoughts. The adrenaline was frying my mind, and my hands and legs were shaking almost out of control.

"Now sit here a minute. And don't faint, dammit" was all Ray said, and he was gone, crashing through the store. In a minute he was back with a big first aid kit, pressing gauze against my neck and putting a cold pack on my forehead.

May June called for him from the front seat of the car, and he went to her. I could hear them talking, but I couldn't make out what they were saying, and then I felt the blood oozing out through the gauze on my neck and running down my back, and the ringing started in my ears and the little silver specks started floating in front of my eyes and—sorry, Ray—I fainted.

I woke up in my own house, stark naked in my own bed with a heavy bandage on my neck and one around my right hand. It was daylight, birds were singing outside my bedroom window, it was hot as hell in the house, and the digital alarm clock beside my bed read 10:44. A shower was out of the question, so I brushed my teeth, splashed some water under my arms and over my face with my left hand, combed my hair, and walked to the diner.

The whole time, I kept thinking of Naomi. Seeing her sitting next to me in the car, confessing her fear that I would reject her—what a ridiculous thought!— seeing her trying to hide the tears that were coursing down her cheeks as she spoke. And then seeing her head hit the windshield and hearing that little muffled scream as she collapsed to the floor of the car.

I have always been a believer in nonviolence. I was a conscientious objector during the Vietnam War, not because I was afraid but because I honestly, sincerely did not believe that violence solved problems. I never struck my children. Not once. I didn't believe in spanking. I had signed a petition when I was a teacher, advocating the abolition of corporal punishment in schools, believing that beating even the worst, most insolent student would only make things worse. I did not believe in violence.

Until now.

Now I wanted to do some extraordinary violence. I wanted to find the man responsible for the fear I had seen in Naomi's eyes last night, and I wanted to beat him until there was nothing left to beat. I wanted to see that same fear in his eyes, and then I wanted to see it dawn on him that there was no escape, no hope of reprieve, no mercy.

"How's Naomi?" I asked again.

"She's fine," May June said, flipping the toast. It sizzled on the griddle and smelled sweet and delicious. "She's got a right smart bump on her head and a whole host of little cuts and scratches. And she's gonna be powerful sore for a few days, what with all those bruises and all, but she's a right strong woman. She'd make a fine wife—"

"Mother," Ray cut in. "Not now, okay?"

"Well, I just thought I'd remind him."

"You don't need to remind me," I said, smiling at her. It hurt my face. "I'm convinced. Where is she?"

"She's sleeping back in the spare room. It was our

boy's, and we never got around to changing it," she said.

"I didn't know you had a boy," I said, trying not to sound surprised.

"He died in the war" was all she said. But she didn't seem upset or overly grieved. Boys die in wars and get their names put on the memorial in Perry, and that's the way it goes. It's sad but you can't let it ruin your life. You grieve and you move on.

"I'm sorry." That was all I could think of to say.

"So are we. He was a fine boy. We'll be healed of it one day, I suppose," she said.

Life is hard. You expect it to be otherwise, and the grief can kill you.

"Can I see Naomi?" I asked.

"Seein's about all you can do. I gave her some of my special tea, and she'll be sleepin' a good while yet."

Ray snorted. "She put a Valium in a cup of sassafras tea." Then, to her, "Some granny woman you are."

She slapped his arm affectionately. "Now, you hush or I'll lose my reputation as a wily old mountain woman."

"Can I have another cup of your special mountain coffee that you buy in a can at the Piggly Wiggly in Perry?" Ray said, grinning at me.

She walked down the counter to get the coffee pot and came back to fill our mugs.

Ray reached into his shirt pocket and pulled out a little envelope, opened it, and dumped the contents on the counter in front of me. About twenty little metal pellets rolled across the counter. "Bird shot," Ray said. "That's what took out the back window." He picked up one of the BBs and studied it. "Don't know what it was that went through the side window, but I'd say it was probably a twenty-two. Anything bigger would have blown out the glass instead of puncturing it like that."

I studied the BBs and nodded.

"You wanna tell me about it?" he prodded gently.

May June slid the toast and honey in front of me and sprinkled it with powdered sugar. I gave my arteries a passing thought and dug in. I thought while I ate, giving my mind time to put it all in the right order. "Ray, I've preached some good sermons and some terrible ones, but I've never preached one that made someone want to kill me." I paused for a moment and reconsidered. "No, that may not be true. They may have wanted to, but they never actually tried it before. This is a first for me."

Ray nodded and sipped his coffee. He started his cigarette ritual to let me know he wasn't in a hurry and said, "Take your time."

I started with our ride back and the detour through Viper. I left out Naomi's and my discussion but included the fact that we'd stopped the car for a moment, and he raised his eyebrows. I finished with the chase down the mountain and my race to Baird and fainting in the rocking chair.

Ray crushed out his cigarette in an ashtray May June had provided, and she whisked it away, dumped it into a can behind the counter, and replaced it immediately.

"You recognize the truck?"

"No."

"Color?"

"It was dark. The lights were in my eyes, and I was scared, Ray. Dark is all I can say."

"When did it start following you? Exactly."

"Well, I don't know for sure. At first we just thought it was another car on the road, so we didn't take much notice."

"You think you put it out of commission? For good?"

I shrugged. "I just got away from it. That's all I was interested in."

Ray sipped his coffee and grimaced, poured a ton of sugar into it, and said, "Well, it's probably gone by now anyhow."

"Ray, why would someone want to kill Naomi? The snake was for me, okay? That I can pretty much guess, even though I don't know why. Hell, I've only been here a few days! But that was Naomi's car. Someone was trying to kill her. Why?"

"Search me. It still could have been you they were after. Someone who knew you'd be up at her place yesterday. You tell anyone?"

I smiled at May June. "No. Too afraid of a scandal. But anyone could have seen us leaving the reception. Thanks, May June. It was a fine reception, by the way, and the cake was delicious."

"Thank Dora Musgrove," May June said. "She baked it. Wouldn't have it any other way."

"So that narrows it down to anyone who was at the reception yesterday," Ray said. "Anyone else you can think of? You make any enemies back in Louisville, hate you enough to follow you here?"

"I didn't even make any friends," I said. "Much less enemies."

Ray grunted. "There is one other group who might have known."

"Who?"

"Naomi's brothers and her daddy. Hebe put you with me, and he don't like me one bit. He could have sent the boys up there to kick your skinny little citified butt."

"No way," I answered. "Naomi was in that car. They wouldn't hurt her, would they?"

"Don't know. Maybe they figured her for a traitor to the family."

"I can't believe it."

"Well, there's only one way to find out for sure." He took another sip of his coffee and stood up. "We'll just have a little talk with 'em. You said yesterday you didn't want to go along. You changed your mind?"

"I reckon I have," I said.

Funny, when you're around people for a little while you start talking like them.

Ray was taking Clark Mountain the way he always did—about twenty miles per hour above sanity. I held on with both hands, leaned toward him to hear what he was saying, and talked as little as possible. Every time I opened my mouth it filled with dust.

"I talked with the coroner this morning. Just like we thought, there weren't much for him to go on. Still, he had a little something." Ray kept taking his eyes off the road as he talked, and every time he did it I winced.

"What'd he have?" I asked, watching the road for him.

"Ernestine died of smoke inhalation—'nough lung tissue for him to tell, I guess. Mac didn't. Died of something else. Doc didn't know what, though."

"How long?" I yelled over the Jeep's abused muffler. I discovered that I did much better speaking in sentence fragments and contractions while riding in Ray's Jeep.

"Before he knows?" Ray shrugged and glanced at the road, then back at me. "He sent some tissue samples to the state police lab in Louisville. Probably two, three weeks."

"What? In a murder investigation?"

"Louisville's a big city. They got better things to do than worry about some ignorant hillbillies who get burned up in a house fire." Now he was looking straight at the road, and the tops of his ears were turning red.

"Still," I shouted, "the lab tests could prove you were right. They could show he was murdered."

Ray just shrugged and changed the subject. "I forgot to congratulate you. You're a rich man."

"How so?" I asked, stumbling after his train of thought.

"I talked to Percy Mills."

I let my face register a question. Who?

"Percy Mills. That old lawyer in town. Martins had a total of $32,404 in savings, their house, their acreage, and their car. It all goes to the Baird Methodist Church. Congratulations!"

"Save it," I said, not one bit excited.

"I thought that would be good news," he said, puzzled.

"I'm just the preacher, Ray. I got nothing to say about how the church uses its money. I can't even vote. Besides, parishioners love to fight over how to spend their money. The more they got, the more they fight."

Ray nodded enthusiastically as I talked. "Already started," he said. "I told May June, and she wanted

187

to air condition the parsonage and buy new rockers for the nursery and fix the bell in the steeple so's it'd ring again. I wanted to pay off the second mortgage."

"Wait until a committee gets hold of it," I said. "The gloves will really come off. We won't have a minute's peace until it's all spent. Probably lose ten percent of our members over it, no matter how it goes."

Ray grinned and looked over at me. "You been around, haven't you, Preacher?"

"Three times and back," I said, smiling back at him.

We drove the rest of the way in silence, and I noticed how the anger was seeping out of me the farther we got up the mountain. By the time we pulled into the Taylor place I just wanted to hit something or someone, one good pop. Death was no longer on my agenda. Sometimes even a little time will heal you more than you realize. I hoped it was healing Naomi.

No one answered the door at Hebrew Taylor's big Colonial house. Ray knocked three times and rang the bell twice and, after a prolonged silence, swore.

"He could be anywhere. The mine, the sawmill, or anywhere on the mountain. Hard as hell to find him, much less Adam," he said, scanning the yard. The only vehicle in the driveway was the dune buggy. The big dog was still sitting in the shade beneath it and didn't bother to come out and bark at us. I didn't blame him. The temperature was just over a hundred degrees on the porch.

"Might as well look around back," Ray said, and started off the porch.

The little pole barn was closed up, a big padlock hanging from the hasp on the drive-through door. The backyard was empty. Hebrew Taylor's lawn chair still sat facing the garden. I wondered where his pet snake, Tut, was, and an involuntary shudder ran up my back and under the bandage on my neck as I looked around the grass at my feet. No Tut.

We started back to the Jeep and had taken about three steps when he heard a loud metallic crash come from inside the pole barn, followed by an oath and a second voice whining. Ray raised his eyebrows and we approached the building quietly.

Up close we could see that the padlock on the drive-through door wasn't engaged. It was hanging from the hasp, but not through the bolt, and turned so it would look locked from all but a few feet away. We stood at the door and listened to the conversation from within.

Voice: Motherfucker! Will you hold the son of a bitch up like I showed you? Jesus Christ!

Whine: It slipped, Benny. I'm sorry. I can't see too good. My head hurts.

Voice (mimicking the whine): My head hurts. I can't see too good. Goddamn! Just hold the motherfucker, okay? Is that too goddamn much to ask? Now lean on it when I tell you. Okay.

(Another crash and the sound of grinding metal.)

Voice: Motherfucker!

(Loud thump.)

Whine: Oh, shit. What're we gonna do, Benny?

Voice: We can't do it like this. We're gonna have to take the motherfucker somewheres.

Whine: Oh, great. And what are we gonna pay for it with? If it's gone more'n a day Daddy'll find out and skin us both.

Voice: Okay, fine. Fuck it! We'll back it out and use a chain to yank it out. That's the only way it's gonna come.

Whine: He'll see, Benny. He'll see it's all fucked up, and he'll know.

Voice: Goddammit, Adam ...

Bingo!

Ray threw the drive-through door up, and it rolled smoothly, if noisily, onto its track near the ceiling. The garage was flooded with light, and we saw the two boys standing at the front of a red Ford pickup truck.

"Havin' some trouble with your truck, boys?" Ray said. He walked slowly beside the truck, dragging his hand along the fender, and nodded for me to do the same on the other side.

Adam Taylor was on my side, standing in front of the pickup, a puzzled expression on his handsome face. He was about my height, six feet or so, but about thirty pounds lighter. The mustache was just as the motel lady had described it: hardly worthy of the name. The Reds cap was on the tool bench behind him.

Benny, his friend, was another story. He would have been comfortable on the defensive line at Ohio State. He stood a head taller than Adam and weighed a good sixty pounds more, all of which was located in his belly, chest, and shoulders. He wore a John Deere cap and bib overalls so old they were nearly white.

Both of them needed a shave and smelled of old alcohol and stale tobacco.

"Hey, Ray," Adam said, trying unsuccessfully to sound casual. "Whatcha doin' way up here?"

Ray walked up to the bumper, and I paralleled him on the opposite side of the truck. Both boys stood where they were. Ray and I were blocking their exits around the pickup. The big tool bench pressed against their backs. "I'm bird huntin'," Ray said, smiling.

Adam made a nervous attempt at his own smile, but it just wouldn't work. "Bird huntin'?" he said, trying to laugh. "What kinda birds you huntin' this time o' year?"

"Peckerwoods," Ray said, straight-faced. He was two feet from Benny who, I noticed, was holding a crowbar in his right hand. "Redneck peckerwoods," Ray said again, looking straight at Benny. "Couple of them were seen over to Mount Devoux last night. Drivin' a pickup and fuckin' with two of my best friends."

"Oh, hey," Adam said, shaking his head. "We wouldn't know nothin' about that. Me and Benny was up by the mine all last night drinkin'. Ain't that right, Benny?"

Benny said nothing and didn't take his eyes off Ray's face.

"That how you fucked up the front of your daddy's truck, here?" Ray asked, nodding his head at the front bumper of the truck.

Adam tried to laugh. "Yeah. Yeah. Ain't we a coupla idjits? Tried to drive down the mountain and put ol' red here into a tree. Hey, you won't tell Daddy, will ya? We was just tryin' to fix it."

Ray shook his head slowly. "I don't think you can fix this, Adam. And I don't think your daddy can fix it, either. Your sister's in the hospital fighting for her life," he lied. His hand moved just a little, and he pointed at the truck without looking at it. "This the truck, Reverend?"

I had told him that it was dark and I probably wouldn't be able to identify the truck, and I was right.

I really couldn't swear in court that this was the truck. But Ray seemed to know what he was doing here. "Yeah," I said. "This is the one."

"Adam," Ray said, "you are one sorry piece of work. I'm sorry, boy, but I gotta say this. You got the right to remain silent...."

Benny swung the crowbar.

No doubt, if we had been out in the open, in the yard or even in a saloon, Benny could have taken Ray. He was bigger, heavier, younger, and he had the crowbar. But we weren't in the open. We were crowded into that barn, and Benny was cramped between the truck and the tool bench and he didn't have room to make a really good swing.

Ray moved faster than I ever would have thought possible for a man his age and size. He didn't duck or try to get out of the way. He just stepped forward, inside Benny's swinging arm, chest to chest with the big kid, and brought his arm up like a piston. The heel of his hand caught Benny under his chin, and I heard the bone break from where I was standing, ten feet away.

Benny went down like a three-hundred-pound sack of potatoes.

Adam screamed like a girl when he saw his friend fall, and turned toward me. He was like a trapped animal, wounded and threatened, and I could see in his panicked eyes that he fully intended to run right over the top of me if he had to to get out of that barn.

He exploded into me, but I had had a split second to prepare for it. I bent my knees and opened my arms wide, the way my high school football coach had taught me. We met chest to chest, and I straightened my legs, letting his momentum carry us up instead of back. I locked my arms around his so his hands couldn't get to my face, but the top of his head crashed into my chin and rattled my jaw.

It hurt, but not enough to make me forget my anger at what he had done to me and his sister the night before. I let out a scream of my own, bent my knees again, thrust upward, and lifted him off the floor, turned, and slammed him down on the hood of the pickup truck.

I heard the wind explode out of him when he hit, so I unlocked my arms from around him and pulled back my right hand to hit him. One good pop in the face was all I wanted. To feel his nose flatten under my fist.

But something caught my wrist, and I nearly dislocated my shoulder trying to throw the punch. Ray pulled me back from the pickup and patted me on the chest. "He's done," he said. "Let me have my talk with him, and then you can beat him six ways from Sunday for all I care."

We Protestants have, by and large, given confession and the sacrament of penance little attention. It's never been a weekly thing with us, confessing our sins. Usually we just throw in a sentence or two at communion time, once a month, and we don't think too much about it: "We acknowledge that we have done those things which we ought not to have done and we have left undone those things which we ought to have done...."

That kind of covers it all.

Even our Roman Catholic brothers and sisters have been playing the whole thing down of late, preferring discussion groups, euphemistically called sharing groups or koinonia groups, over the dark little cubicles where the faithful once communicated in protected silence with their confessor.

Philosophers and theologians have said over and over again throughout the ages that deep down inside we really do want to confess our shortcomings. We want to blurt out all those ugly things about ourselves that only we know, so that we don't have to carry them around inside us. We want to be totally known so we can be totally loved, and the only way we can accomplish this is in confession.

So, they say, confession is not only good for the soul, it is also necessary. People want to confess.

Don't bet on it.

Even trussed up and lying in the sun outside the pole barn in Hebrew Taylor's backyard, Adam Taylor and Benjamin Kneeb did not want to confess.

We had hauled them out there, and Ray had fashioned some very serviceable manacles out of some hose clamps he found on the tool bench. The two boys lay on their sides, back to back, fastened securely to each other at the wrists and ankles. Benny had come to while Ray and I were looking over the pickup truck. He had jerked a couple of times and Adam had let him know immediately that it was not only futile but painful to make such violent motions.

"God damn, Benny! You're gonna cut my damn hands off you don't quit jerkin' around. Shit!"

Ray and I had walked out into the sun to hear their confession, but neither of them was in a confessing mood. When Ray bent over to look at Benny's broken jaw, the big guy mumbled something like, "Hmuck-oo!" and jerked his whole body to give the phrase added emphasis.

"Jesus, Benny! Will ya lay still, fer chrissake!" Adam screamed to his companion.

Ray walked around to Adam and bent over to look at his face. "Now you wanna tell us why you took off after your own sister like that last night?" Ray asked gently.

"My daddy's gonna come home and kick your ass he finds you treatin' me like this" was all Adam had to offer.

Ray looked at me, smiled, grabbed Adam by the lapels, and sat him up straight. It must have taken a Herculean effort, because Benny was fixed to Adam in such a way that when Adam came up, so did Benny, both of them back to back and screaming, their position so awkward as to make my own ankles and wrists ache just from watching them.

"God damn! My daddy's gonna kill you. Look what you done! My wrists are bleedin'. I can feel 'em. You're a dead man, Ray Hall."

Ray slapped him. Open palm, right across the face. Adam started to fall back over, taking Benny with him, but Ray caught them and propped them back up.

"Shut your face and listen to me, you snot-nosed, pimply-faced little shit," Ray said quietly, threateningly. "You're in more trouble than a one-legged man in an ass-kicking contest, and I don't care your daddy's Jesus Christ come again, there ain't nothin' he can do to help you."

"We ain't done nothin'—"

Ray slapped him again. Not hard, just enough to sting his face.

"Boy, you got diarrhea of the mouth or what? You keep interrupting me when I'm tryin' to talk. Now, listen to what I'm sayin'." He held up his hand and ticked off his fingers as he spoke. "Attempted murder, hit and run, dangerous operation of a vehicle, speeding, assault with a deadly weapon, carrying an open container in a vehicle, driving under the influence." He stopped and looked at Adam. "Am I getting your attention, boy? I'm talkin' 'bout jail here."

Adam's jaw had dropped down to his chest, and he was beginning to look worried. Ray just crouched there looking at him, waiting for an answer. Sweat began to pop out on Adam's forehead and run down his nose. His eyes darted back and forth.

"It was Benny," he said at last.

Benny jerked his hands hard, and Adam screamed. Ray ran around and looked Benny straight in the face. He drew back his hand and brought it around so fast I hardly saw it, and I heard Benny whimper. Ray's hand stopped a millimeter from the boy's broken jaw. Benny's eyes were closed.

"You just stay like that," Ray said and stepped back around to where he was facing Adam. "Now, what were you gonna say?"

"It was Benny, Ray, honest. We was drinkin' up to the mine, like I told ya, and I guess we got a little drunk." Adam was talking fast. Ray sat down, cross-legged, in front of him and listened intently. "So we decided to drive over to Viper and have us a little fun with that ol' crazy man.

"Well, Jesus, Ray! We no more'n pulled up there and the crazy guy comes runnin' out into the street with a shotgun, wavin' it around and sayin' to leave him alone and stop fuckin' with him."

Ray's eyebrows shot up. "What?"

"Well, he didn't say 'fuckin',' like that. He was just yellin' about how he didn't want any trouble and we should stay away from him and all. Christ, Ray, he's crazy as bat shit. I don't know why you let him live up there."

"I tell you what, Adam," Ray said. "You don't tell me how to be a constable and I won't tell you how to be an asshole. What happened after that?"

"Hell, whadaya think happened? We got the hell outta there. But ol' Benny, he's pissed, see. So we pull off the road and back into the bushes at the cutoff, and Benny says we're gonna drink some beers and wait until dark and go back and get that ol' crazy man. Ram that shotgun up his ass. Make him think twice before he starts wavin' it around again."

Adam stopped as though he was finished.

"Well?" Ray said, prodding him. "What happened?"

"Ray, it's awful hot out here in the sun. Can't we move over to the shade, there? And these damn clamps are cuttin' into my wrists somethin' awful."

"Adam, are you bein' cute with me? 'Cause if you are—"

"No, hey, honest to God, Ray. I'm just askin' is all. It ain't no big thing."

"Good. Then you won't mind puttin' up with it a bit longer while you tell me what happened last night."

"Oh, sure," Adam said, nodding, wanting to be helpful. "Well, nothing happened. I mean, we didn't go back to Viper to get the old crazy man because, directly, here he comes, zipping outta the Viper cutoff fast as hell."

Ray sighed and started to get up. "Adam, you know damn well that wasn't any crazy man."

"Well, sure I do, now, Ray. Hey, sit down, will ya? Sure I do now! But last night we'd been drinkin' some beers, you know. And we just see this car go shootin' by, and Benny, he's behind the wheel, he says, 'There he goes. Let's get 'im.' Like that, and the next thing I know we're bashing into this car goin' down the mountain.

"Well, Benny, he's laughin' and I'm scared shitless,

and next thing I allow as how this car looks kinda familiar, but what with all the beer and all, I can't remember where I seen it.

"So, next thing you know, this car is stopped and Benny's tryin' to push it off the mountain, and I think, Jesus H. Christ, that's Naomi's car and then it shoots off and Benny, he stalls the truck and then, *pow!* Sombitch hits us and takes off, and I figure, shit, ain't no way that's Naomi. But by then he's gone and Daddy's truck is all fucked up."

Ray stood up and looked at me, a question in his eyes. I shrugged. Could be.

"Where's LeAnn, Adam?" Ray asked, abruptly changing the subject.

"What? Hell, Ray. How the hell should I know?" Adam looked at me as though I might back him up.

"You change the place you take her? You got some other little love nest besides the Sawyer Motel?" Ray was pacing back and forth now, not looking at Adam.

Adam kept looking at me. "Oh, hey, Ray. That was just, you know. Fun. We weren't serious or anything. We's just havin' some fun's all."

"Where is she now, Adam?"

"I don't know, Ray. I swear to God!"

"You didn't take her off somewhere after she burned down the Martin place?"

"Me? No, hey. I don't know nothin' about that."

"When was the last time you saw her?"

"Thursday. I drove over to the old mill on Pine Tree Mountain Road, and she walked down from the Martin place to meet me. I was on my lunch hour, and she brought some stuff for us to eat. We sat in my truck and ate."

"She show you her titties, Adam?" Ray looked right

at him. "I hear she's a good lay, boy. That true? That little white-trash slut cop your honker for you?"

Adam's face turned crimson, and the muscles in his neck knotted. "Don't you talk about her that way, God damn you. You an' my daddy are just alike, talkin' about her that way when you don't know a thing about her. She ain't like that. She's a ..." He was breathing rapidly, and a realization came over him.

"You get awful upset for a boy who was just havin' some fun with the town floozy," Ray said. "Where is she, Adam? You two fixin' to run off somewhere? She hidin' somewhere waitin' for you?"

"I don't know where she is!" he shouted. "God-damn, I looked everwheres. She was supposed to meet me at the old mill that night, but she wasn't there. So I drove up the mountain to the Martin place. It was on fire. At first I figured she was dead, but then ..."

"You the one called in the fire?" Ray said, kneeling down next to the boy.

Adam nodded. Tears appeared in the corners of his eyes. "I can't find her, Ray. God knows I've looked everwheres. We was gonna get married."

Ray took a screwdriver out of his back pocket and walked around to where Benny had been sitting silently, listening. He pointed the screwdriver at Benny and shook it gently. "I loosen those hose clamps on your wrists, you promise to be a good boy?"

Benny was turning pasty gray and sweating more than the summer sun could account for. I began to wonder if he was going into shock. The pain in his jaw had to be enormous. He squinted up at Ray and I could see the hard anger in his eyes. He was making a valiant effort to be tough, but it was costing him.

Then, abruptly, the eyes softened. He nodded his head very gently and squinted at the pain that it caused.

The boys stood and rubbed their wrists and ankles but looked sheepish. "Ray, you ain't gonna tell Daddy 'bout this, are you?"

Ray looked at me and shook his head. "Adam, I guess that's up to Naomi and the Reverend, here. It was them you hurt."

Adam dropped his eyes to the ground. "Yeah. How's Naomi doin'? Can you tell me her room number?"

"She's at my house, Adam." The boy's head shot up in surprise. "She's banged up and cut a little, but she'll be okay. You stay away for a day or so then come talk to her. Your daddy gonna be expecting her?"

Adam shook his head. "Naw, she usually comes and goes as she pleases."

"Okay, then. You boys stay outta trouble if you can. I expect you're gonna have to come up with a pretty good story to explain the truck and Benny's jaw, here."

"We'll think o' somethin'," Adam said, a worried look crossing his face.

Ray started his cigarette ritual and talked as he tamped it on his lighter. "Just one more thing, boy."

"Sir?" Adam had changed his song since our arrival. Sir, indeed.

"What's all this about a crazy man livin' over to Viper?"

Adam looked at Benny, then at me and back at Ray. "He's been there for a coupla weeks now, Ray. Livin' in one of the buildings they boarded up."

Ray lit his cigarette. "Yeah, I understand that. But

what's he got to do with all this? Why'd you decide to go messin' with him last night?"

Adam looked at his shoes. "He's her daddy, Ray."

"Whose daddy?"

"LeAnn's. That ol' man is Zester Bertke, her daddy."

Ray shook his head and turned toward the Jeep. "Christ," he said to no one in particular.

Ray walked back into the diner and sat down in front of the biggest ham sandwich I had ever seen, made even bigger by two half-inch slices of tomato. The sandwich in front of me was only a little smaller. Both of us had a cold Budweiser and at least a pound of potato salad as well. May June was mashing eggs and cracker crumbs into ground beef in preparation for the Monday night special, meatloaf.

"Jerry's not home," Ray said. "Gone to Perry for groceries or some damn thing."

Ray had wanted to eat and talk to Jerry Sites before we went up to talk to Zester Bertke. He had hoped to find out if there was anything else we should know before facing the crazy, snake-handling, poison-drinking, shotgun-toting preacher.

"I think Adam probably told us everything he knew about the guy," I said around a mouthful of ham sandwich. "He didn't seem to know a lot."

"Mmm."

"I wish I'd have known you wanted to talk to Jerry," May June said. "He stopped by for his mail this morning, and when I told him what happened he insisted on going in to see Naomi. He seemed real bad upset that she had been hurt. I heard 'em talkin' 'bout Viper, and I think they had a prayer together."

I felt an irrational surge of jealousy at the thought of good-looking, charismatic Jerry Sites praying with Naomi Taylor. I tried to dismiss it, but it wanted to hang around and jab at me.

I had tried to talk to her immediately when I got back from the Taylor's, but she had just finished her lunch and, I suspected, another cup of May June's special tea, and she could barely carry on a conversation, much less say a prayer.

I kissed her, and she grabbed my neck with more strength than I would have thought possible. "You know what'd make me feel a whole lot better?" she whispered in my ear.

"What?" I answered.

"A nice long soak in the hot tub." She giggled, and then she was asleep, snoring softly. I kissed her again and went out to my mountain of ham on whole wheat.

"Anything else happen while we were gone, Mother?" Ray asked May June.

"Well, LeRoy Whiteker called and said everything was set for the funeral tomorrow. I okayed the obituary for the paper in Perry. Was that all right, Dan?"

I assured her that it was fine. She knew the Martins better than I did and was perfectly qualified to approve the obituary notice.

"And Hebrew Taylor called and said he wanted to report a coal truck that ran his boy Adam off the road last night. Can that be right? Do coal trucks run on Sunday nights?"

"They do if Hebe Taylor says they do." Ray smiled. Obviously the boys had come up with a story that Adam's daddy could, or at least would, believe.

There were three dinner invitations for me, which May June had politely put off, using the Martin funeral as an excuse. And my mother had called.

"What a pistol she is," May June said mysteriously. "We had quite a nice talk."

"What about?" I asked, trying to sound unconcerned.

"Why, about her favorite son, of course. And her grandchildren and her garden and, oh, a lot of things. She wants to know when you're gonna invite her down to hear you preach."

I shook my head. I had been in this church less than a week, and my mother was already preparing to come down and make her evaluation.

"Well?" May June said. "When are you gonna invite her down?"

"Soon," I said.

"Which one is it you're ashamed of, Dan. Us or her?" May June giggled. She had an infectious giggle that let you know that she was just having fun and that you were not to take her seriously.

"Mother, for God's sake," Ray said.

"Oh, I'm just teasing," she said, slapping his arm. She went back to her meat loaf.

Ray had finished his sandwich and his potato salad. He took another swig of beer and lit a cigarette. "Tell me about crazy preachers," he said.

"What do you want to know?" I asked.

"What makes 'em crazy? Why do they do the things

they do? What should we expect when we go up to talk to him?"

"You want me to go with you?" I asked, trying to sound surprised. Actually, I was elated. I was so involved in this thing now there was no way he could have kept me away.

"Well, I figured the two of you might speak the same language," he said. "You two both being preachers and all."

"Ray, saying that Zester Bertke and I are alike because we're both preachers is like saying two people are alike because they both come from Kentucky. There are preachers and there are preachers. You know what I mean?"

"So what kind is he?"

"Well, he's a Fundamentalist. Uneducated. Emotional. He takes every single word in the Bible and says that it is the absolute truth and should be followed word for word."

"Like this business of handling snakes and drinking poison?"

"Exactly," I said. "And that's the worst part. The passage that snake handlers quote as their authority isn't really even in the Bible. At least, most scholars don't include it. It's from an obscure ending to the Book of Mark that most people think was added later, long after Mark was dead and gone. You got a Bible around here?"

"Mother?" Ray said in May June's general direction.

"In your office," May June said, not looking up from her work.

Ray left and was back in a minute, carrying a battered Revised Standard Version of the Bible.

"What, no King James?" I asked, looking over the old book.

"Don Merriweather was a progressive," Ray said, seriously. "Onliest thing he would use was the RSV. Got him in some hot water at first."

"Good for him," I said, thumbing through the book. "Here it is." I read from the footnoted longer ending of the Gospel of Mark: "Chapter sixteen, verse seventeen: 'And these signs will accompany those who believe: in my name they will cast out demons; they will speak in new tongues; they will pick up serpents and if they drink any deadly thing, it will not hurt them; they shall lay their hands on the sick and they will recover.'"

"He thinks he can do all that stuff?" Ray asked.

"No, he knows he can. He's seen it done, and he's done it himself."

"How? How's he managed to do it without getting killed?" Ray asked. His face reflected more curiosity than disgust.

"He uses defanged snakes, or he milks them before he uses them in a service. Or he chills them and makes them lethargic so they don't strike. Or he keeps them full. A snake that's just eaten doesn't usually bite unless it feels threatened. Some of these guys also drink small amounts of poison over a long period of time and build up a tolerance for the stuff. Some just slowly poison themselves to death by letting the toxin build up in their systems."

"What about the healings?" Ray asked. "Has he done that?"

"Who knows?" I shrugged. "If people genuinely want to be healed, sometimes they can be. Or they can be convinced that they're healed, at least until they get home that night. If they aren't healed by a miracle, then it's not the preacher's fault, it's their own fault for not having enough faith. Same thing if they get bitten by a snake and die. Well, obviously they didn't have enough faith. It's a test."

"Sounds like a con game to me," Ray said.

"Sometimes it is. A guy comes along, handles a few tame snakes, takes up an offering, and splits. Other times, though, it's a local sect, and the stuff goes on for years. Or until someone gets bitten and dies. Then usually the authorities move in and put an end to it. If a preacher truly believes, though—and I'll bet Zester Bertke does—he can justify anything he does to make snake handling work."

Ray was shaking his head in disbelief.

"Don't try to make it make sense, Ray. It doesn't. We're not dealing with a rational man, here. If nothing else, the fact that he raped his own nine-year-old daughter would prove that."

"I reckon," Ray said. "Lord, what a crazy religion. It's hard to believe that this guy is in the same family as guys like you and Donny Merriweather."

"We like to think of men like Bertke as the black sheep of the family," I said, and tried a smile.

Ray didn't smile.

He walked into his office and came out holding his .410 single-shot shotgun.

"I guess we better go talk to him," he said, and walked toward the door.

"What I want you to do is talk Jesus to him," Ray shouted as we drove up County Road 3 toward the Viper cutoff. "Can you do it?"

I nodded. I could do that. Talking Jesus, as Ray put

it, wasn't really my style, but I could do it. In my prime, before the great fall, I had been the guest preacher at more little churches and more big gatherings than I could count, and all of them had had their own expectations of what a good sermon was. And every time, I delivered a good sermon. Many times it was better than good.

You want grand oratory? I could give it.

You want folksy homily? I could preach it.

You want hellfire and brimstone? I could deliver it.

You want me to talk Jesus? Talk I would. If Zester Bertke had killed the Martins to get his daughter back, as Ray suspected he had, talking Jesus might be the only way to get her away from him. It might be the only language his twisted mind could understand anymore.

So I would talk Jesus.

What I didn't understand, though, was why Bertke had tried to kill me with the snake in the picnic basket. I asked Ray as much.

"Didn't know it was you," he shouted over the roar of the Jeep. "He just knew it was the parsonage to the Methodist church and it was the Methodist preacher who took his little girl away and threatened to whip his ass if he didn't git."

"What if he doesn't want to talk?" I asked after a while.

Ray nodded to the little .410 gauge shotgun lying in the backseat of the Jeep. He could say more with a nod than most men could say with a speech.

Viper was like a tomb.

The gravel road that dissected that town threw up clouds of dust around the Jeep as Ray parked it in the center of the street, and we sat quietly, listening. June bugs buzzed around the tall grass and crumpled buildings on either side of us, and somewhere far away a rooster crowed, but that was all. Sweat ran down my forehead and stung my eyes.

"Well, let's do it," Ray said, climbing out of the Jeep. "We'll leave the gun and try talking first."

I didn't like the idea of leaving the gun, but before I could say as much, Ray was walking down the middle of the street, slowly looking at either side. I trotted up next to him and walked beside him for about ten strides, not really knowing what we were looking for.

We heard the first shot before we felt it.

An explosion erupted from somewhere at the other end of the little ghost town, and Ray dropped immediately to the ground and, almost as quickly, knocked my legs out from under me. I came down on my butt and heard him shout, "Cover your head!"

I did, just as the buckshot rained down on top of us. It stung, but it didn't really hurt. I looked to my right, and Ray was gone, crawling backward, crablike, toward the Jeep. I followed on my stomach.

Another shot and we stopped and felt the metal rain again, this time with less impact. Ray stood and sprinted to the Jeep, me right behind him.

We ducked behind it, and Ray shouted over the top, "Reverend Bertke, we're just here to talk! We don't mean you any harm. I'm Ray Hall, township constable, and I got some questions—"

A third shot. This time it was a full three seconds before the buckshot sprinkled down on the Jeep.

"Shit!" Ray said, ducking behind the hood.

"Now what?" I said, thinking of the gun in the backseat.

"Well, at least we know where he is."

"We do?" I said. "Where is he?"

Ray peeked over the top of the Jeep and pointed to an old building still nearly intact about a hundred yards away at the other end of the little town. "The old church," he said. "Bottom left-hand corner of the first window."

Another shot and Ray didn't even bother to duck. "We're outta his range. He's just playin' with us now." He reached in and drew the .410 from the back of the Jeep along with a box of shells, broke it open, inserted a shell, and filled his pockets with about twenty more. "I guess he's set the rules. We'll have to play it his way."

"Does this mean I won't have to talk Jesus to him?" I asked, trying to smile.

He looked at me and deadpanned. "Don't run off. I may need you yet." He peeked back over the top of the Jeep and looked around. "Oh, shit."

"What?"

"Store's closed. Margie usually opens on weekday afternoons."

"Maybe she heard the shooting and decided to keep her head down," I suggested.

He shook is head. "Nope. Sign's on the door. She hasn't opened today."

"Maybe she went out of business."

"Not that store," he said. "Selling cigarettes, gum, candy, and pop to the folks around here isn't much of a living, but it's all she's got. That and the shine she sells out back. No, she oughta be open." And with that, he dashed out from behind the Jeep, running in a zigzag pattern to the only other fully standing edifice in Viper, a little wood frame store with rusty tin roof and a Dr Pepper sign on the front.

Not liking the thought of being left alone in the street, I followed.

Two more shots rang out from the church as we ran, and I covered my head both times, hoping Bertke was still using the shotgun. I couldn't help thinking about the neat little holes in the side windows of Naomi's car. The ones made by a bullet, not by buckshot. A bullet fired from a rifle or a handgun.

I collided with Ray and nearly knocked him down as I rounded the corner of the store. We were now about fifty yards from the church and on the opposite side of the street.

"Margie lives in a little Airstream behind the store," Ray said. "See if she's home. I'll make sure that the good Reverend doesn't go anywhere." He stuck his arm and the shotgun around the side of the building and fired off a shot in the general direction of the church. It was immediately answered, and I walked to the back of the building.

The Airstream trailer was about twenty feet long and as many years old. The bald tires had long ago succumbed to dry rot, and the trailer now sat balanced on concrete blocks. Someone had tried to paint it, but the dark green paint had not adhered to the aluminum, and brush strokes could easily be seen all over the surface. The paint itself had thinned on the shiny surface and run down the side, pooling at the bottom of the walls and on the ground below.

The grass was knee high, brown, and alive with June bugs, buzzing in crazy circles around me as I waded toward the door. Only when I got there did I realize that a narrow path led from the trailer to the back door of the store, which was padlocked. The door of the trailer was ajar. I should have taken that as a warning.

She was dead, of course.

The coppery, cloying, sweet smell of blood was strong when I opened the door, and I could almost taste it when I stepped inside. It was at least 120 degrees inside the trailer, and flies were thick and deafening. Margie—I did not learn until later that her last name was Monroe—had been killed as she ate breakfast. Eggs and grits.

A shotgun.

Blood, brains, bone, eggs, and grits were spread over the table in equal portions. She had been sitting in the little booth, looking toward the kitchen, away from the door, and he had simply stuck the shotgun through the opening and pulled the trigger only a couple of feet from her head.

The walls, the little yellow curtains at the window, the ceiling, the table—everything in the trailer seemed to be covered with blood. A three-foot puddle of it was dried on the floor, and it was teeming with flies.

My ears began to ring, little silver specks started to flash in front of my eyes, I began to sweat profusely, and I dashed from the trailer into the shade of the store just in time to lose my lunch. I slid down the wall and sat there with my head between my legs, slipping in and out of consciousness. I was vaguely aware of the ineffectual gun battle going on just a few feet away from me, but I heard little of it for some time. What brought me around was Ray's voice.

"Dead?" he asked.

I nodded.

"Bad?"

I nodded again and felt my head spinning.

"How'd it happen? Could you tell?"

"Shotgun," I murmured. "From behind. While she was eating. Oh, Christ." I leaned to the side and tried to throw up again, but there was nothing left to come up.

Ray handed me his handkerchief, and I wiped my face and looked up at him.

"You gonna be okay?" he asked

I nodded again. "Yeah. It was so hot in there," I said. "The flies. Why didn't I hear them before I went in? There must have been thousands of them."

Ray nodded toward the yard. "June bugs. You thought you were hearing June bugs."

Of course. The damn June bugs sounded like helicopters. I had just shut my mind off to them. I looked back up, but Ray was walking away. He broke open the shotgun and a spent shell flew nearly over his head. He replaced it with another and held two more in his left hand. The shotgun he held waist high, the stock resting on top of the two shells in his hand.

I had seen my father do this when I was a kid and he had taken me pheasant hunting. It was the way you held your gun and shells when you expected to reload quickly. With practice, a man using a single-shot could pull off three shots almost as quickly as a man using a bolt-action repeater.

Ray stepped around the corner of the building and yelled: "Zester Bertke, you crazy son of a bitch! You put down that shotgun and come out of that church or I'm gonna kill you. Do you understand me? You've killed enough people!"

Nothing. No answer. No gunshot.

Just the sound of the June bugs ... or the flies. I didn't want to know which.

I don't know why I followed Ray Hall down that street. Lord knows I didn't want to. My head ached from puking, and my legs trembled, and my stomach was rolling over like a Ferris wheel. I kept seeing the bodies of Margie Monroe and Mac and Ernie Martin, and I didn't want to think about what might have happened to LeAnn Bertke if that maniac in the church had been holding her for the past four days.

Come to think of it, that was probably the thing that pushed me up onto my feet and down the road toward the church. I just kept seeing the face of LeAnn Bertke in that high school picture, refusing to smile, looking tough and seductive at the same time. And that picture kept melting into the other, younger version, taken when she was nine years old, the right side of her face bruised and swollen. I kept seeing that damaged little girl as she waited and listened and cried into her pillow as her crazy father came down the hall to rape her again and again until the two preachers showed up one day and rescued her.

I just kept seeing that little girl cringing back in the corner of her room. And then I saw her growing, the bruises on her face healing, but the wounds on her mind never quite mending. Never trusting another man. Flashing her breasts for rides up the mountain. Spreading her legs for a ticket out of Appalachia. Riding along on her life instead of steering it, because a crazy man had given it such a violent push early on that it could never be in her control again. A crazy man who called himself a minister of Jesus Christ.

"Let the little children come unto me, for to such belongs the kingdom of God."

Somehow he had managed to miss that one. He'd found one obscure passage about picking up serpents and drinking poison, and he'd fixed on it and he'd never gotten around to the real stuff of Christianity.

And I hated him for that.

I hated him and his religion and his church and his hollow goddamn ignorance. And when Ray Hall marched in there and stuck that shotgun up his ass and pulled the trigger, I wanted to be there.

So I followed.

And Ray led.

And about twenty yards from the front door of the church another shot rang out.

We both dropped, instinctively by now. But this time there was no buckshot. I looked at Ray and he pointed his finger at me, thumb pointing skyward. He lowered his thumb, like a child shooting an imaginary enemy.

The shot had been fired from a handgun. Inside the church.

We sprinted toward the front door of the church and stood, our backs to the wall on either side of it. Ray reached out, turned the knob, and eased the door open.

Silence.

Slowly, quietly, he crouched down and duck-walked around the corner and into the church, the shotgun pointing the way in front of him. I waited outside, sweat pouring off of my face. Finally I heard his voice echoing inside the building.

"Take a deep breath before you come in," he said.

A church like any other. Maybe a little poorer than most, but not so poor as you might think.

Salmon pink walls with crude murals of biblical scenes.

Pews facing forward toward a small chancel. An altar in the middle, against the rear wall. A small lectern from which the Word would be read. A larger pulpit on the right where the preacher would preach.

And Zester Bertke slumped over the pulpit, draping it as though he were protecting it from something about to fall on it from above. Blood dripped from the right side of his head onto the floor. A revolver lay at the foot of the pulpit beneath his hand where he had dropped it.

And, of course, the snakes.

Probably twenty-five or thirty of them. In boxes, in bottles, in jars. A few dead ones, lying on the floor at various places. Timber and diamondback rattlers. Every one of them deadly.

Ray shot them all. Loading and unloading the shot

gun, walking slowly around the church and dispatching them with cold efficiency, while I sat in a pew and tried to make some kind of sense of it all. The hate was gone, replaced now by absolute bewilderment.

On the wall to the right of the chancel was nailed a snakeskin. The markings were the distinctive gray-green diamonds of the diamondback rattlesnake, and this one must have been a record setter at nearly six feet in length. Above it was spray-painted a sentence from the long ending of the Gospel of Mark: "They shall pick up serpents."

On the other wall, beside the lectern, was a picture of LeAnn Bertke, blown up to poster size. She was about twelve years old in the grainy black-and-white photo, and she was smiling a thin, forced smile. Her dress was a frilly print that would have looked better on a child half her age, without the budding figure and the mature, knowing eyes. And she looked to be wearing hose and pumps that might have belonged to someone much older than she. Neither child nor adult, she looked exactly like what she was. Confused.

Above the picture was painted another obscure biblical quotation: "Fallen! Fallen is Babylon the harlot!"

Ray walked up to me and said something, but the blasts of his shotgun had set my ears to ringing and I could not hear him. I didn't really care. I had something else on my mind.

"She's dead, isn't she, Ray?" I asked, already knowing the answer. "He killed her, didn't he?"

Ray nodded.

"Where do you suppose he buried the body?" I asked, not really expecting an answer.

Ray shrugged and walked out of the church. He

patted my shoulder as he left. Take your time, it seemed to say. I'll wait.

He didn't have to wait long. I wiped the tears from my face with the sleeve of my shirt, blew my nose on Ray's handkerchief, and left.

My God, my God, why did you forsake her?

Rex Littlejohn was the guy who got me through the first funeral of my career.

I was three weeks out of seminary, and the deceased was the ninety-odd-year-old father of one of the five angry women who ran my first church. Rex was a big man, well over six feet tall who looked thin from behind. His suit pants were impeccably cleaned and pressed but baggy in the seat. He had, as far as I could tell, no butt at all.

Seen from the side, he looked pregnant. He had a beer belly that seemed to extend a full foot beyond and above his belt without sagging even an inch. His suit coat was tailored to close over his girth, but he never closed it, probably out of habit formed in less prosperous times. He was clean-shaven, completely bald, and smelled strongly of English Leather.

He was a serious bass angler, a fair golfer, a moderate drinker, a talented storyteller, and the best, most scrupulous, most sensitive funeral director I have ever met.

He knew without asking that I had never presided over a funeral, so he took me into his office, poured me a cup of coffee, and gave me the short course: "Keep it short. Keep it positive. Let the Word do the talkin'. Read the old familiar stuff; this ain't the time to teach progressive theology.

"Preach to their hearts, not their heads. Don't say

anything that ain't true or that you can't prove. Don't make promises that you can't keep. You ain't a preacher right now, Dan. You're a pastor. Them folks need hugs more'n they need words. So keep your words short and your hugs long.

"Oh, and watch me. Anything goes wrong or seems like it's gonna, you watch me. I'll tell you what to do."

I might have been offended if anyone else had told me that stuff—another preacher, maybe. But Rex Littlejohn was just too real to get mad at. He looked me right in the eye when he said that stuff, and I believed every word he said.

And I still do.

The funeral for McHenry and Ernestine Martin was scheduled to begin at ten A.M. on Tuesday, and folks started arriving at nine thirty. LeRoy Whiteker had arrived at nine and placed the closed caskets at the front of the church with a respectable number of bouquets.

By nine forty-five the temperature was close to 85 in the church and hotter outside, threatening to reach well over 100 by the end of the day. Honeybees had smelled the funeral flowers and were coming through the open windows for them, but the heat seemed to be too much for even them. They buzzed around more out of habit than out of any real interest in nectar.

By ten o'clock the sanctuary was about half full, and Dora Musgrove began the pre-service music. Old familiar stuff that everyone knew and expected: "In the Garden," "The Old Rugged Cross," "When the Roll Is Called Up Yonder."

Ray and May June had waited on the porch, hoping

to catch a breeze until the music started, and they came in. Naomi followed, smiled shyly at me, and sat next to May June about a third of the way down the aisle. She was wearing a plain brown cotton dress that only let you guess about her figure, but made the guessing fun. Her face was still bruised and scratched, but even that couldn't hide the glow that radiated from her eyes. It made her look rugged and vulnerable at the same time. Does that make sense?

Like—yes, I've been through it, but I've been through worse and will do it again if I have to because that's the kind of woman I am. That kind of look.

I'd seen it before, of course. LeAnn Bertke had it. All three of the pictures I had seen of her had shown that same kind of tough vulnerability. Beauty hidden beneath cuts and bruises. And other Appalachian women, too. And even some of the men had it.

Ray had it.

Even now, as he sat in his pew, bags under his eyes, exhausted and depressed, I could see that look in his face: This is bad, but I've seen worse, and I'll see worse yet.

But how could it be worse?

Yesterday I had finally gotten my legs to work and walked out of the Pentecostal church into the street only to find the ghost town of Viper deserted. The Jeep was still there, but Ray was gone. I started to panic for a moment and shouted his name several times before he answered. He had broken into the store and used the phone to call the sheriff's office in Perry.

It took them nearly two hours to get there, and we spent the time sitting on the front porch of the store, drinking soda and smoking. We didn't talk except to ask if the other wanted another pop. Once I took a leak around the side of the building. Mostly we waited.

Sheriff William B. Fine arrived. Took our statements and dismissed us. He would take over now. Later that night Ray called the sheriff's office and asked the only deputy on duty to read the report to him.

Sheriff Fine had discovered some official-looking papers in the old church. Zester Bertke, they said, had been released from a mental hospital in Nashville three weeks earlier, no longer considered a threat to himself or others.

Somehow, the sheriff reported, Zester had managed to make his way to Viper where he took up residence in the old church and lived off of soda and cheese crackers he bought from Margie Monroe's store. When his money ran out, he had killed Margie and, when cornered, himself.

That was it. The Martin murders, the attack on Naomi and me, and the snakes in my kitchen and the school locker were not mentioned.

"Asshole," Ray said as he hung up the phone. "He doesn't see a connection. Can you believe it?"

"After what I saw today, I would believe anything," I said.

"Everything nice and neat. No need to open up all this other stuff now that the killer is dead. Just leaves a lot of unanswered questions." Ray drank half of his beer and slammed the can down on the countertop. "God damn!"

I sipped my beer and belched. It was my third, and I was beginning to feel sleepy. "Like how did he do all that running around without a car?" I asked.

"Yeah," Ray said. "Where's his car? How'd he get up to the Martins' and over here and up to the school without being seen if he didn't have a car or a truck?"

"And where's LeAnn?" I said, starting to feel sad again.

"And why'd he kill himself?" Ray said. "Why the fuck did he shoot himself?"

"He was crazy, Ray."

"He was religious crazy. Do religious crazies kill themselves?"

"They did in Jonestown."

"Bullshit!" He slammed his beer down again. "Some of them, maybe, but not all of 'em. They had guns to their heads."

"Maybe," I allowed.

"Damned right."

I left it at that, walked home, took a shower, and went to bed. The beer had helped me sleep. Without it I would have been a lost cause, what with the heat and the pictures that kept floating through my mind—snakes and guns and stained glass.

Even as I sat there in front of the congregation, waiting to start the funeral service, the visions kept floating back to me.

A sad-faced little girl with the right side of her head swollen and bruised.

A snakeskin nailed to the wall of a church.

A poster-size photograph of that same little girl, but now the bruises were on the inside and you could only see them if you looked deep into her eyes.

A battered, broken old man slumped over a pulpit with blood dripping from the right side of his skull.

And snakes. Dozens of them, exploding. And the smell of cordite and old shotgun shells.

And June bugs. Hundreds, thousands of them, crawling all over the inside of the trailer ...

Silence.

Everyone in the church was looking at me, waiting. Dora had finished her music, and it was time to begin the service. I stood in the pulpit, cleared my throat, and began by introducing myself.

"It was not my good fortune to know Mac and Ernie Martin in life, but in death I have come to know them well," I said, in all honesty. "Their friends are many, and each one has a different story to tell about Mac and Ernie. Yet there is a sameness to all of the stories, and that sameness is love.

"Mac and Ernie loved well and often. They gave birth to no children, yet they were parents to many. They owned little, yet they never hesitated to share what they owned. And when their lives were ended, what they had they gave away without any strings attached." That was the money the church would inherit. No strings. They had said that in the will: "to be spent as the pastor and administrative board decide by majority vote." Bless both their hearts, they were true Christians.

From there I followed Rex Littlejohn's advice. I kept it simple and short.

Opening statements of comfort.

Readings from the Psalms and Paul's letters.

And a short homily.

My text for the homily was taken from Psalm 73, verse 13. I took it slow and easy, breaking it down into its component parts, talking briefly about each:

Nevertheless ...

I am with thee ...
Continuously ...
Thou holdest me ... .
By the right hand.
It was on the last phrase that my eyes met Ray's
and he dashed from the church.

"Shoot yourself," Ray said as he entered the diner. "In the head."

We had just returned from the graveside service up at the cemetery on Pine Tree Mountain, and May June was fixing a poke salad—dandelion greens, I later learned—and thick meat loaf sandwiches on home-made bread. Naomi and I sat on stools at the counter, drinking Bud.

"Sit down and have some lunch, old man," May June said, paying him no attention. "Where'd you run off to? I had to make some mighty fancy excuses, don't you know. I just told them you was overcome with the heat."

Ray ignored her as she did him and repeated his request. "Go ahead," he said, a smile just beginning to form on the right side of his mouth. "Put your hand up to your head like you was gonna shoot yourself."

Dutifully, Naomi and I complied.

"I'll do no such foolish thing," May June said, not

turning from her salad preparations. "That's the stupidest thing I've ..."

"Right handed, aren't you?" Ray asked, nodding his head enthusiastically.

Naomi and I lowered our right hands and nodded. We were both right-handed. So?

Ray took a picture from his shirt pocket and tossed it on the counter. It was the Polaroid of LeAnn Bertke that had been taken by Jerry Sites and Donald Merriweather when she had arrived at the Mountain Baptist Children's Home, her face swollen and bruised.

"Now, which hand did Zester Bertke favor?" Ray asked, tapping his finger on the picture.

We both leaned over and looked at the old photo. It had faded considerably since being reintroduced to the air outside Jerry Sites's filing cabinet. Naomi saw it first.

"The bruises are on the right side of her face," she said. "That means her father hit her with his left hand."

"Unless he backhanded her," I added.

Ray was shaking his head vigorously. "No. Hell, Dan, you backhand a kid once, maybe twice, but not over and over again. To get that kind of bruising, you'd have to hit her maybe ten, fifteen times. And remember what Jerry said? Her right arm, shoulder, and ribs were bruised, too."

I had to agree, it looked pretty convincing. "So Zester Bertke was left-handed. What's that got to do ..."

Ray was smiling bigger than I'd ever imagined possible. He was also pointing his own imaginary gun at his temple. His right temple. "Zester Bertke didn't shoot himself. Someone wanted us to think he did and botched it because he was in such a hurry. He shot ol' Zester in the wrong side of the head."

"But who?" Naomi said.

"And why?" May June added, delivering our salads.

"I'm not sure I got it all figured out yet," Ray said, taking a seat at the counter. "But I'm close."

"Well, you gonna tell us who done it or you gonna just sit there and gloat like a banty rooster all afternoon?" May June chided.

"I'm not tellin' anyone until I get a call I'm waitin' for," Ray said. "That's why I got up and run outta church like that," he added to me. "Was your sermon that done it. 'He holdeth me by my right hand.' Got me to thinkin' about the right hand and that bein' the one you always just sort of assume people use to do important stuff with. Leastwise that's what he thought when he shot Zester."

"He who?" May June nearly shouted. "Who was it killed that crazy preacher?"

"No one killed him, Mother. Calm down. Ol' Zester died of snakebite. Musta been dead several hours by the time we got there. Wasn't Zester was shootin' at us at all. And wasn't him shot Margie Monroe, either. I called the coroner in Perry when I left the church, and that's what he said. Snakebite. Diamondback, most probably, though Zester had enough other poisons in him to kill a man twice his size. He was drinkin' the stuff, too."

"Oh, Lord," May June said, and fanned herself with her apron.

"What's this phone call you're waitin' for?" Naomi asked, taking my hand.

Ray noted our hand play and nodded approvingly.

"You two keep that up and we'll be havin' little preachers runnin' around here before you know it."

Naomi stuck her tongue out at him, but he didn't see her. The telephone was ringing back in his office, and he was off the stool, nearly running to get it.

"Look at that," May June said around a mouthful of salad. "Man his age runnin' in this heat. Give himself a heart attack, he's not careful. Don't know how a phone call could be so ..." She stopped in midsentence, and her hand came up to her mouth. "Oh, Lord."

Naomi and I had to look over our shoulders to follow May June's gaze, and I saw the color drain out of Naomi's face before my eyes focused on the doorway of Ray's office.

Ray was backing out of the room very slowly, and Jerry Sites was walking with him, facing him, unshaven, hair uncombed, sweating. He was holding a brown snake in his right hand, the diamond-shaped head gripped tightly between his thumb and forefinger. The snake's body was wrapped around his arm, up to his shoulder. Uncoiled, it probably would have been a little under three feet long, but its diminutive size did not comfort me.

I had seen its mate coiled on my kitchen table—same small size, same color, same hourglass design on its back.

The phone rang eight times and stopped. I can remember thinking, insanely, that eight times wasn't enough.

What I said was a question: "Copperhead?"

Jerry Sites nodded and looked at the snake, then back at Ray. "From under the porch up at the home," he said. "Been keeping it for a special occasion. Got it before Darnell took the others away."

"What you figurin' to do with him?" Ray asked quietly.

Jerry looked at the snake again, as though he wasn't quite sure what he planned to do with it. His shoulders slumped for a moment, and then he looked back at us with complete contempt and anger.

"Well, I don't know what the fuck I'm supposed to do now!" he exploded. "You came back too damned fast! I waited until you made your phone calls and left, then I was just gonna sneak into your office and leave him for you in your desk drawer or something.

"But, oh, Christ, no." He looked at me. "Mr. God Almighty quick-as-a-flash here couldn't stretch out the funeral a few more minutes. He had to come in with his whore and Mrs. Hall and trap me in that goddamn closet you call an office. Jesus!"

"It's awful hot in there, I know, Jerry," Ray said, backing away from the snake. "Maybe you'd like a little iced tea or a beer or somethin'. Mother?"

"Listen to him!" Jerry said, smiling. "Jerry, he calls me! In all the time I've lived here has he ever called me Jerry? Fuck, no, he hasn't! Reverend Sites. Reverend Goddamn Sites! That's what he calls me. And always with that little inflection in his voice like he doesn't really believe I'm a minister. Like it's a joke or something." He stepped toward Ray and thrust the snake toward him. Ray leaned back but didn't run. "Well, fuck you, mister. The joke's on you!"

"Reverend?" May June said, and Jerry and I both turned toward her. She looked straight at Jerry and held out a large tumbler of iced tea. "Would you like a cool drink? I brewed it fresh this morning in the sun."

"Thank you, Ms. Hall. You're a decent and kind woman." He stepped to the counter behind Naomi and took the tea. As he lifted it to his mouth I looked at Naomi and her eyes shifted to her right, away from the counter. Could she move fast enough to give me a shot at him with my beer bottle? I looked at Ray, and he shook his head almost imperceptibly. Maybe if it was a knife or even a gun, but you don't mess with a live snake. You never knew where it would end up or who it would be mad at.

Jerry carried his tea to a chair and sat down. He was exhausted, but he took care to keep the snake held tightly and away from his body.

"So how much have you got figured out, Ray?" he asked, slouching into the chair and running the cold glass across his face.

"Well, you killed Margie Monroe. And you probably killed LeAnn Bertke and the Martins. And you tried to kill Reverend Thompson, here, though I'm not sure why." Ray sat in a chair about six feet away from Jerry, facing him. "Mother," he called to May June, "can I have a Budweiser, please?"

She complied immediately.

Jerry Sites smiled sadly and shook his head. "Well, you got part of it, at least. I heard that much from back in the office there. And, yes, I'm the one who was shooting at you yesterday in Viper."

"Why me?" I asked, and caught a quick glance from Ray. Stay out of it, he seemed to say. Let him forget you're here.

"You? I wasn't trying to kill you, you silly shit! That other copperhead was meant for that stupid little bitch who calls herself a wife. Jesus, doesn't anyone see a pattern in any of this?"

No one said anything, and Jerry got more exasperated. "She was a whore! She was a conniving, blackmailing little whore!" he screamed.

"Rachael? Your wife?" May June said, shocked.

"No!" Jerry slammed his hand on the table, and iced tea sloshed over the rim of his glass. "Goddamn! Don't you people listen? Rachel isn't a whore. She's just a stupid little Ohio hillbilly girl who's got religion. But she isn't a wife, either. Won't even sleep with her own husband!"

"LeAnn," Ray said evenly.

"Yes! Yes! The little whore! Zester was right. Babylon the whore. That was her all right."

"She was blackmailing you?" Ray asked.

"Not at first. At first she was just fucking me. God, I felt awful. I was supposed to be her guardian and take care of her. I even turned her over to Rachael to keep her away from me, but Jesus, it was as much me as it was her. She'd sneak up to the house and do it in my room while Rachael slept in the room next door, or I'd go down to the dorm late at night and meet her out back and we'd do it in the grass on a blanket. God, that girl could screw.

"She knew things I'd never dreamed of. Ol' Zester may have taught her, but she was an apt pupil, I'll say that."

Ray took a swig of beer and burped. "Then Zester showed up, right?"

"Yeah. Fucked up everything," Jerry said, shaking his head. "We were supposed to get married. I was gonna leave Rachael, and LeAnn and I were going to get married."

He turned toward me and snarled. "Don't get your ass in the air, Reverend. She's legal age in this state, and I would have done right by her, the little whore." He took another drink of tea and went on. "She called me and told me to meet her at the old sawmill at the bottom of Pine Tree Mountain. Said it was really important.

"I thought this was it. She was ready to go with me. So I told Rachael I was going to Perry, and I went to meet her. You know what she wanted? She wanted money! Her daddy's back, she says, and she's scared of him and she wants money so she and that Taylor kid can go off and get married! It's him she's in love with. All those times she's been running away? She's been going off with him and fucking his brains out!

"She says that if I don't come up with three thousand dollars she'll tell everyone about us. My wife, my career, everything'll be down the drain and all I'll have to show for it is a set of blue balls! Christ, she had a mouth on her."

"So you killed her to save your career. Why'd you kill Mac and Ernie, Jer ... Reverend Sites?" Ray asked.

"It all went wrong," Jerry said. He stretched his arm, and the snake moved. He watched it as it writhed slowly along his skin. "I was supposed to bring the money up to the house that night. Mac and Ernie were supposed to be gone to a revival in Perry.

"I was so fucking mad! I got Darnell to help me catch one of the snakes from under the porch. Then later I put it in an old gym bag with some newspaper. And I drove back up to Mac's place to give it to her. When she reached in there, she was going to get what she deserved. Venom for venom. Poison for poison.

Besides, snakes won't bite the righteous. Isn't that what her daddy said?

"But when I pull up into the yard and get out of the car, there's Mac, coming out of the door to greet me. Couldn't go to the revival because Ernie's got a migraine headache. Isn't that a hoot? She wanted to go to the revival to get healed of migraines by this evangelist who's supposed to have the gift of healing, but she's got a migraine and she can't go." He started laughing, chuckling to himself, and continued for three full minutes until I thought he had lost the thread of the story, but he started again.

"Anyway, Mac sees the satchel and asks what's in it, and I told him it was just some of LeAnn's stuff she'd left down at the home. By this time LeAnn's standing on the porch, and she's worried as hell, and I'm lovin' it. Only Mac, he grabbed the bag and tried to take it away from me. Said he'd better have a look inside, see, just to make sure it wasn't illegal contraband. He was teasing LeAnn, you know.

"He grabbed and tugged and I didn't let go and he tugged a couple of more times, and then, before I know what's happened, he's yanked it away from me and opened it, and I guess that snake was mad at being thrown around like that, because it came straight out of that bag and hit him right under the chin. Just sort of hung there."

Jerry reached over and stroked the head of the copperhead in his hand. The forked tongue of the snake shot out like lightning. Jerry's voice was getting quieter and sadder.

"Mac panicked and slapped the snake away and ran toward the house and collapsed in the doorway. LeAnn saw the whole thing, and she panicked, too.

Started screaming like she was crazy. Goddamn! Why can't anything ever go the way you plan it? Your career, your marriage, your life, your plan to kill your mistress. Nothing is ever easy, is it?

"I was just so fucking mad, that when LeAnn started screaming I hit her. Then I hit her again, and again, and again. I guess I killed her. There were some chains in the back of the truck and I wrapped her in those, drove over to the Viper Quarry and tossed her in. That's where she is, now, Ray. Bottom of the quarry. Never find her. Too deep. Too big."

"We'll find her," Ray said, still looking into his beer bottle.

"I went back to the house because I realized that my clothes were covered with blood and there was probably blood all over the porch there, too. And there was. Too much to clean off. So I found some cans of gas in the shed and poured them around the house and set it. I guess I just forgot about poor old Ernie sleeping in there."

"I guess you did," Ray said. "Why do you suppose she didn't wake up with all that screamin' and what have you goin' on the front yard?"

Jerry sighed. "Migraine headache, Ray. She went to bed with a migraine headache. Mac said she took three of her pills."

"Darvon," May June whispered. "She was takin' Darvon. Three of 'em woulda put her out like a light. She never heard . . ." She held a dish towel up to her face and waved her hand at the room.

"Can you figure the rest out?" Jerry asked. He seemed to be getting more and more exhausted with the telling of his story.

"I guess you tried to kill Rachael with that snake because you were tired of her," Ray said.

"No, I didn't really want to kill her. I just wanted to scare her. Did that, didn't I?" He laughed. "Christ, wet her pants right there in the Methodist preacher's kitchen. I just kept seeing the look on ol' Mac's face when that snake came flying out of that bag, and I wanted to imagine that same look on Rachael's face." He chuckled again. "I'd have given a hundred dollars to have been there. I was sitting in the shadows across the road and heard the whole thing. I nearly died. It was great.

"Oh, don't worry, Dan. I'd been keeping that snake in the refrigerator. It was so cold and lethargic it would hardly move when I put it in the basket. See, I watched Darnell catch the first one, and I caught a couple more myself in case I needed them." He stroked the snake's head again. "This one here was in the fridge, too. Only she's been out a good long while now. And I think she's kinda hungry, too. Aren't you babe?"

"What about the one in the locker?" I asked.

"Wasn't me," Jerry said, and shrugged his shoulders as if that was all that needed to be said.

"That was Zester," Ray said. "It was a rattler, remember? Somehow he managed to get into the school and put one of his favorite snakes in her locker. Had her name right on it so it wasn't hard to find. That's how I knew something was wrong.

"All the snakes in the Pentecostal church were rattlers. Zester had a thing for 'em. Not one copperhead in the bunch. But your snake was a copperhead. That's what that call was." He nodded toward his office. "I called the lab in Louisville and told them to test for copperhead venom in McHenry Martin's tissue samples. The fact that they called back means they found what they were looking for."

"Mac wasn't killed by Zester Bertke if he was killed by a copperhead."

"Bravo!" said Jerry Sites. "Sherlock fucking Holmes has done it again."

Ray went on as though Jerry had not spoken. "Jerry came down here to get his mail yesterday and Mother told him what happened to you and Naomi in Viper. He went in to talk to Naomi and got the whole story, found out there was someone livin' in Viper that mighta seen him dumpin' LeAnn's body. What took you so long to get to Viper, Jerry? You found out about Zester in the morning, but you were still up there when we got there after lunch."

Jerry's eyes popped open. Had he almost fallen asleep holding a snake? "Rachael had the fucking truck! Had to wait until she got home. Only beat you there by a half hour."

Ray nodded. "So you went down to make sure no one saw you dumpin' LeAnn's body, right? Leave no witnesses?"

"A sound policy, though Christianity would have suffered greatly had it been put into general practice," Jerry said. He was sounding drunk with fatigue.

"He shot Margie in her trailer and found Zester dead in the church just as we were pulling into town. Fired off some shots to keep us away and make us think Zester was still alive. Then he put one into Zester's head, propped the body over the pulpit and slipped out the back of the church, rolled his truck down the hill until he was outta earshot and made his way back home. We couldn't hear him 'cause I was shootin' all them snakes. That it, Jerry?"

Sites nodded, beaten.

"Well, it was quick thinkin,' Jerry, I'll give you that. But it was a sorry plan. I would have put it together sooner or later. Too many flaws."

"What flaws?"

"Slips of the tongue, poor planning. Like how would a man who was dead from snakebite shoot himself with the wrong hand in the wrong side of his head? And how did you know on Sunday that Mac Martin was going back into the house when he died? All anyone said was that his body was found on the porch. I checked with the Carmack twins. They hadn't talked to anyone about it. And the snakes. Why copperheads when Zester Bertke only used rattlers? I called Nashville, Jerry. He had a fixation with rattlesnakes. See, it was just a matter of time before I caught you."

Jerry's eyes flew open again. "Bullshit. You're a hick cop in a hick little town in the middle of nowhere. No one even gave a shit but you. You think your cousin is gonna believe that the Baptist minister, administrator of the children's home, really did all this stuff?"

"I got witnesses to your confession," Ray said, nodding toward Naomi and me.

"No good. You didn't Mirandize me. Can't use my confession in court." He smiled drunkenly.

Ray smiled, too. "Mother heard me Mirandize you, didn't you, Mother?"

May June nodded.

"Reverend? Naomi?"

We both nodded.

Jerry Sites's eyes filled with fury and he started to rise from his chair, but Ray moved first.

"No!" Jerry screamed. He made a heroic effort to stand, but he was clumsy and slow. He looked as if he hadn't slept in two days, and his face was sweating heavily. He stumbled, swayed, and his eyes rolled up into his head.

Naomi and I jumped from our stools and backed away from him just as Ray reached him and clamped a huge hand around Jerry's hand and the snake's throat.

Jerry was breathing deeply and crying, but he didn't resist. Ray peeled the snake out of the Baptist preacher's hand and clasped its head and throat in his own fingers. Slowly he unwound it from Jerry's arm and lifted it away.

May June was by his side, and he handed Jerry over to her. She lowered him back into his chair. "Just sit down for a spell, now, Reverend. You just relax here. Put your feet up." She pulled another chair over and lifted his feet up onto it.

"So tired," Jerry mumbled. "Haven't been able to sleep. Kept seeing her when I closed my eyes."

"Yes, yes. I know. You'll sleep now. My tea has that effect on folks. Helps 'em sleep."

Jerry Sites's eyes rolled as he tried to focus them on May June's face. "You drugged me?"

"Just some of my special tea to help you relax," she said, patting his arm as he drifted off. She straightened up and looked at Ray, who was still holding the snake. "Would you please take that thing outside?"

"How much did you give him?" Ray asked.

"Only a little. Just ten of these little Valium but he only drank half the tea. Five was enough, as tired and hungry as he was." She combed her hands through Jerry's hair and patted his face. "Poor thing."

Ray shook his head. "Mother, you're a fine granny woman, but you'd make a terrible cop. That poor thing right there has killed four people in the last week."

She made a pshaw gesture. "You never did like him," she said, walking back around the counter and collecting the half-eaten salads. "Now take that snake out of here and I'll get you a sandwich. You'd better call Billy. This is the sheriff's business now."

"Already did. Called him this morning and told him something was gonna happen," Ray said, walking toward the door. "Said he'd be out after lunch."

Naomi squeezed my hand to keep me from laughing. "After lunch?" I said, not believing.

"That's what he said," Ray hollered from the porch. "Little numb-nuts peckerwood ..." His voice was drowned out by the sound of his boots clomping down the steps.

20

Sheriff William B. Fine, a spidery little man with an Alfalfa haircut and horn-rimmed glasses, arrived with two of his deputies while Naomi and I were up at the children's home, breaking the news to Rachael Sites.

Rachael had gone home after the funeral to read her Bible and had grown sleepy in the afternoon heat. We found her in her underwear on the couch, her Bible open on her chest. The pages were wet with perspiration.

No, she hadn't seen Jerry in a while, but she had been at church a lot, getting ready for the opening of Sunday school on Labor Day weekend, and sometimes that happened. Since they slept in separate rooms now, she hadn't realized that his bed had not been slept in.

Was she upset? Well, a little, maybe, but not really surprised. She wiped a few tears from her face as she explained how Jerry was not, after all, a born-again Christian and she had known for a long time

241

that the devil had a firm grip on the Reverend Gerald Sites.

"How do you mean?" Naomi asked.

"Well ..." Rachael rolled her eyes. "You know!"

Naomi and I looked at each other and shrugged.

Rachael sighed. "Sex!" she whispered. "He wanted to do it all the time!" She shuddered. "Oh, yes. Satan had a firm hold on him. That's why I moved out of his room. You could just see the evil in him whenever he looked at me. Lust! That's what it was. Lust, pure and simple. All he ever thought about was his ... thing.

"That's why Satan is depicted as a serpent in the Bible, you know. To warn us. Didn't you ever notice how a man's ... thing looks like a serpent? Well, there you are. It's an instrument of Satan! It makes a man crazy. Makes him think of ... other things, not of Jesus. And women, too. Women can become slaves if they think about it too much."

She clasped her hands to her chest and raised her eyes to the ceiling. "Jesus, I just want to thank you for freeing me from that evil man and the temptations he held before me. Be kind to him, Lord, and don't send him too deep into perdition on account of it wasn't him that done those terrible things; it was Satan in him, and he ..."

Naomi was dragging me out of the house by the hand, and I didn't hear the rest of Rachael's prayer.

"Sitting there in her underwear talking about the evils of sex!" Naomi said, fuming. "Jesus, Dan, she drove him crazy. She flashed that body in front of him and then withheld it when he showed interest. So he went to LeAnn Bertke." She stopped and whirled around to face me. "She's as guilty as he is. Rachael and her stupid religion drove that poor man crazy."

"Now you sound like May June," I said, drawing her to me, enfolding her in my arms.

"No, it's not that. I think what he did was terrible, but I just wonder if he ever would have done any of it if she had been a real wife to him. Why does religion do that to people?"

I hugged her to me and felt her breasts push against my chest. I kissed her and then began to kiss the scratches on her face. "Not religion," I said between kisses. She closed her eyes and yielded to me, closing her arms around my waist. "Just crazy religion. Crazy people are going to have crazy religion. Ignorant people have ignorant religion."

"What kind of religion did Jerry Sites have?" she asked, kissing me softly.

That one caught me off guard. "No religion, I guess. He had a church and a title and a job. And maybe some rituals and jargon. But he didn't really have any religion."

"It's too hot for this," she said, pulling slowly away from me and turning to walk back down the hill. Then she stopped and winked over her shoulder. "But I know where there's a nice cool hot tub and a couple of cold beers."

I followed her like a puppy.

Four weeks later we held the big Labor Day kickoff for the Sunday school. Picnic on the grounds of the church. Hot dogs, cold soda, potato salad, volleyball, lots of standing around talking and smoking and chewing tobacco.

The District Superintendent showed up and seemed

satisfied that I still had my pants on. He shook hands all around, made a production of eating a hot dog just like a regular Christian person, and generally acted like the ecclesiastical politician that he was.

Naomi managed to drag her father and brothers down off Clark Mountain for the big event and Hebrew even treated me civilly. He still refused to talk to Ray, but I imagined that Ray was happy with that arrangement. Adam had taken LeAnn's death hard and was in no mood to picnic and party. He ate a hot dog and pushed little Isaiah, his five-year-old brother, on a tire swing. I wanted to go up to him and say something but I didn't know what to say. I would try later, maybe in private.

Mom showed up for the weekend and even paid to fly my kids in from California. She picked them up at the airport in Corbin in a big rented Lincoln and only got lost three times trying to find Baird. She and May June spent most of the weekend swapping recipes and talking like two long-lost friends.

At the picnic, Mom managed to fit right into the crowd as though she had been born on Pine Tree Mountain and lived there all her life. When she offered to help in the kitchen, everyone let her and reported to me, later, that she was a wonderful woman of whom I should be very proud.

I am, of course.

On Monday night, there was a dance on the basketball court up at the school. The Carmack twins played fiddles and some of the other folks brought out guitars, banjos, and even a mandolin. Sweet mountain music.

I was dancing close with Naomi when Mom cut in and glided me through the crowd to center court.

"She's young enough to be your . . . niece," Mom said, smirking. "How'd you do it?"

"She was mesmerized by my preaching," I said, trying to look serious. "I seduced her from the pulpit."

Mom just laughed and punched my arm. Then she hugged me close, stood on her tiptoes, and whispered in my ear. "Don't fuck this one up."

Mom's always been a practical person.

MALICE DOMESTIC

Anthologies of Original Traditional Mystery Stories

1

**Presented by the acclaimed Elizabeth Peters.
Featuring Carolyn G. Hart, Charlotte and Aaron Elkins,
Valerie Frankel, Sharyn McCumb, Charlotte Maclead
and many others!**

2

**Presented by bestselling author Mary Higgins
Clark. Featuring Gary Alexander, Amanda Cross,
Sally Gunning, Margaret Maron, Sharon Shankman
and many more!**

And Coming in May 1994

3

**Presented by Agatha Award winner
Nancy Pickard**